SAUL

TATE'S CROSSING BOOK 5

KATHI S. BARTON

This is a work of fiction. Names, characters, places, and incidents are products of the author's imagination or are used fictitiously and are not to be construed as real. Any resemblance to actual events, locations, organizations, or persons, living or dead, is entirely coincidental.

World Castle Publishing, LLC

Pensacola, Florida

Copyright © 2024 Kathi S. Barton

Paperback ISBN: 9798891261624

eBook ISBN: 9798891261631

First Edition World Castle Publishing, LLC, February 26, 2024

http://www.worldcastlepublishing.com

Licensing Notes

Cover: Karen Fuller

Editor: Karen Fuller

Chapter 1

This was the last leg of his eighteen-hour flight, and Saul could not wait to be home and in his own bed. Coming home early would mean that there'd be no surprise welcome home dinner, but he didn't care. At this point, if they'd met him at the airport with a bed, he'd be thrilled beyond anything he'd ever gotten for Christmas and birthday all rolled into one—Damn it, he thought. Saul looked at his ticket and then the seat number that was right in front of him.

"That's my seat." Saul didn't want to get into a big fight with someone. "I have reserved three seats in first class because I deserve it, so please, so there aren't any arguments to ensue, get out of my seat and go find your own." He stared at the man for several moments while he checked his own ticket.

"It was empty when I got on the plane. And I don't want to ride in coach. It's all the way in the back of the plane, and these seats are supper comfy. You're young and fit. Go back there and — why do you need three seats anyway? Just get your ass seated, and no one will know the difference." Saul told him that he would know because they were his seats, and he had paid for first-class seats. The man reached for the woman right behind him, holding what appeared to be ten bags. "Come on, honey. This idiot said that he had reserved three seats. We can sit together without any fuss right now. He's going to be a polite person and go back to coach where I told him and not put up a fuss, aren't you? Now, do as your told, and I won't have to knock the crap out of you. You heard me. Go."

"I'm not going back and sitting in the seats that were assigned to you. So no, you can't sit together. Those are my seats. If you think you can bully me, it's not going to work. You picked your seats when you paid for your flight; now go to them and leave me alone." He signaled for a stewardess, and of course, the man said that he shouldn't have involved her. That he wasn't being the least bit neighborly about this. That the woman had work to do. "Yes, that's why I called her. She's the one to get you two out of my seats."

Saul explained everything to Donna, the woman in the nice crisp uniform. She was pretty, but Saul was just too exhausted to flirt with her at the moment. Mr. Seat-thief, of course, wasn't going to show her his boarding pass either. It was his right or something that he didn't have to do that once he was seated.

"Sir, this isn't yours nor your wife's seat. Please gather up your things and follow me. I'm sorry, Mr. Tate. I'll have this taken care of in a moment." The man said that it was already taken care of as he'd agreed to go to the back and sit in coach. And that he and his wife had done trades with him. He was in his right seat. "However, you're not. Please get up and follow me. The sooner you cooperate with me, the quicker we can get this flight underway."

Saul had had about enough. Tossing his stuff in his third seat, he started picking up the couple's things and setting them in the long-crowded isle. After getting screamed at—the wife actually got into his face and started just screaming at him.

He sat down. Saul was sick of people and their 'I'm entitled to what you have because I want it' attitude.

He tried to tune out what was going on around him. The couple, a younger-looking couple he thought them to be about his age, continued to argue that no one needed three seats and that he was touching their things. Saul didn't point out that they were touching his seats but let it go. For now, at least. He just wanted to lie in his seats and sleep the last four hours of his way home.

He'd been out of the country from home for the past three weeks. While away, he'd been trying his best to get a deal on a building that would hold donated emergency supplies for their country when a disaster happened. The town's leaders, six men who, for the most part, sat around telling him that they already had things set up the way that they wanted them. However, if he had it on them, they'd take the cash so that they could hand it out to people if something like that were to ever happen. Sure, Saul thought.

He was positive that there would be no money set aside for a disaster after they were finished. They weren't cooperating with him at all, so he packed up and was ready to leave on Wednesday evening. He'd had enough.

A tropical storm hit in the early hours of Wednesday morning. It took out most of the electricity on the small island, as well as running water, food, and medical services. Hundreds of people had been killed because there had been no shelter in place. Also, there weren't any supplies on hand they could use because they'd been wasting his time since he arrived.

Doing what he needed to do to help—mostly taking charge of the situation, Saul called in the things that he'd been telling them about, the items that the Tate Foundation could have on hand for them in the event that something like this were to happen. Just like it had before he was leaving.

The towns leaders, jackasses, the lot of them, had argued that his water and other needed items weren't going to help them at all during the next election. The mayor actually wanted Saul to supply him with an endless supply of money that the mayor could distribute where he saw a need. He told him that if he had to give out things, they needed air conditioners for the new building they'd built—that the men had sheltered in with their families while entire other families were washed away — and nice beds so they'd not have to sleep on the floor. They actually complained that it had been too hot in the building. Like having air conditioners would have benefited anyone without there being any electricity on the entire island.

The Mayor had actually got into his face and told him that he could either supply the money so that he could give it out to make him look like his people's hero or they wanted nothing to do with him. They didn't want his supplies coming in without their approval because, apparently, Saul was making him look bad.

Not only did the poor people need the water and other items that he said they could supply, but they also needed a great deal more than he'd first estimated. Medical supplies were in great demand. Also, something that he'd never thought of was body bags.

However, when the Army and National Guard showed up, they were more than happy to use the supplies. And no matter how much the mayor begged them to say that he'd made the arrangements or they weren't going to distribute them, they passed out everything that he could have brought in.

The mayor told his fellow countrymen how he alone had been working on making a deal with their foundation for them to pay for his home, not anyone else's nor the hospital that had nearly been destroyed, to make it a place they could all be proud of. Four nights later, while out shaking hands and asking the people who had nothing left for money for his projects, the mayor had been killed when a wall came down on him and his brand-new car, crushing him as well as his driver.

"Mr. Tate?" He smiled at Donna and noticed that the couple were huffing their way back to the back of the plane. "Everything is ready now. I've had security see to the couple, and I've made sure that your seats are cleaned. Your brother, Joel, I believe he said his name. He told us that you were going to be sleeping and, if at all possible, make sure you have a comfortable journey home."

"I didn't tell them I was coming home. I know that you didn't know that, but how did they know I was coming home today?" She smiled and went away with a small trash bag of what he assumed was cleaning supplies. Reaching out to his brother, he asked him how he'd known. *"I mean, I didn't even tell Mom or Dad that I was leaving there. How did you — let me guess, one of the lovely wives looked it up for me. Nice. But don't expect me to be in the celebrating mood. I'm beyond exhausted."*

"I understand. There are a few things going on around here that we have our hands in that would have made it so no one would have been available to pick you up. This way, we had a handle on it. Loren and Hanna finally have their home finished up. You did get to meet her before you left, didn't you?" He said that he'd not. *"Oh, sorry. They've worked hard with the faeries to get things finished up for them to move in. Also, the funeral is tomorrow for Clarence and Mable Holt. I know you're aware of that stuff going on. Dad told you."*

"He did." Yawning again, he asked if he could tell him the rest later. *"I'm tired. I feel kind of weird, too. Not sick but sore all over. Like I'm getting a cold — which I have never had before. Anyway, I'm going to go to sleep now."* He laid down across the first two seats and put his pillow on the third. He'd have to wake up to buckle when they landed, but for now, he was about as comfortable as he could be.

When he was shaken awake, he didn't have

the slightest idea who was over him nor where he was. Donna, the woman from earlier, told him that they would be landing soon and that he needed to sit up. Nodding, all Saul wanted to do was sleep more. But he did make a half-assed effort in getting up enough to buckle.

"I don't want to be rude, Mr. Tate, but you don't look very good." He said that he didn't feel well either. "Is your family meeting you at the airport? I don't think you should drive home." He said he'd contact his brother and have him drive him home. "I think that's a good idea. I know that you would run warm but you're feeling hot to the touch. I'm going to make sure that no one of your bothers you as the plane disembarks."

He must have dozed off again because the next thing he knew, Joel and his dad were standing over him. It took him a bit longer to realize that he was on a stretcher in the airport and that he was strapped down. Saul was feeling worse than he had before. Like he was on the verge of death or something close to that.

"Dad, I don't feel well." He said that he was aware of that. "I hurt all over. I didn't feel this way earlier, when I left. Now, all I want to do is curl up in a ball and die."

"You don't be saying that to me, young man. You're going to be just fine. I have some people waiting at the hospital who are going to take care of you. You just hang on, son." He looked at his dad's worried face and told him that he was going to be fine. However, nothing in his body or head had him thinking that was a true statement. "You're going to be put in the air ambulance, Saul. You just hold on tight."

Sick now, he was given a smallish bag to throw up in. Christ, he felt like he was being turned inside out. When he felt something pinch him in the arm, it didn't really bother him as it just seemed to be one more bit of pain. Then he felt the medication take him under.

~*~

Lynn watched the man sleeping. He had been this way for the last few days. Mom had been able to save him, even though she'd been told that he couldn't die—no one lived forever, she knew. But her mom had asked if anyone had checked him for bites. She'd run across that once when she'd been doing work on a policy.

"Has he said anything more?" Lynn shook

her head and told her mom when she came back that he'd just been sleeping. "I found out some things that you're not going to believe. And trust me when I tell you, I'm still having trouble with it. This man is a shifter. A wolf. His entire family is."

"No way. They really do exist?" Mom told her how Mr. Joesph had changed his hand into a great big paw and let her touch it. It was soft, she told her. "Wow. Do you think that he'd do that for me one time? I'd love to be able to tell my friends at—I bet you can't tell anyone, can you? That sucks."

"No. You can't tell anyone what I have to tell you. They'll literally kill us if we do. I'm not joking." Her mom looked so serious that Lynn believed her. "Also, there is a queen. I forget what her name is—"

"Aurora." They both looked at the bed that the man was lying on when he spoke. "Do either of you know who I am? I mean, I know who I am. But I can't for the life of me recognize your voices. I'm Saul Tate...right?"

"Yes. I'm Chalina Holt, and this is my daughter, Lynn. We were asked to keep an eye on you while the family went home to get some rest. They've been here nonstop since you were brought in." He asked her mom if she knew what had happened to him. "Yes. You were bitten by a spider. Well, I'm not sure how many there were, but they found three bites on your body. They know what the spider is because one of them laid their eggs into the wound on your shoulder."

"Gross." Lynn laughed at Mr. Tate. "All right. So, I'm assuming that I'm no longer an incubator for the momma. Anything else happen to me while I was out? How long anyway?"

"This is the sixth day." Lynn got up and went to his bedside. "I can give you sips of water, Mr. Tate. The staff told me, but you're to take it slowly. Also, I'm not sure why he thought you needed to know this, but your dad said to tell you that you're not to do anything stupid. Do you usually do stupid things?"

"No, not usually. I'm sore. But I could use some water." She held the straw to his mouth and pulled it away when he seemed to be taking more than she thought that he should. "I understand why you did that, but I'm so thirsty right now. Thank you for making sure that I'm not sick again."

"You have an IV in that is running wide

open. I'm not a doctor, but I'm assuming that they're working on getting you hydrated." Mom looked at her. "Give him another sip, honey, but not too much. We don't want him to get sick on our watch."

She did what her mom told her and then sat down when he said he had enough. Mom pulled out her cell phone and called someone to tell them that Mr. Tate was awake again. Mr. Tate looked at her with his eyes open now and asked her how many times he'd been awake.

"Two today. Once earlier in the morning. And now. You usually don't open your eyes, so this is the first time that you've seen me. My mom and I came out here to Ohio so that I could go to my grandparent's funeral. My grandda was nice, but Grandma Mabel was a terrible person. I guess you might have known that, too. She's the one that killed the principle and that little boy." He said that his dad had told him about it. "They said that they had but wasn't sure if you'd remember or not."

"Your brother Joel would like to speak to you if you can manage it, he said. But if you're hurting, he said that he understood." Mom had to hold the phone for Mr. Tate, but he did talk to his brother.

Crying while talking to his brother, Lynn handed him a tissue when he kept wiping his eyes with his gown. She had to wipe her own tears because he told his brother that he loved him about a dozen times. No one had ever said that to her but her mom. Not even her dad had said that he loved her, even when she was a little girl.

When he was finished talking, he told them how sorry he was. Lynn went into the bathroom and quietly sobbed a little. The man was sorry because he was emotional. That was something that she'd never heard before, either, but from her mom. That someone was sorry.

When she was cleaned up again, she made her way back into the room. Her mom was gone again, having to go to her own room a few times a day so that the staff could check on her foot.

It was a good thing that they'd come here, she thought. Mom had remembered the spider bites and had them check for them, and her foot— having been broken when they'd been home had gotten some infection set in and had to be operated on again. Otherwise, she would have lost her foot.

"How are you doing?" She shrugged and

told him that she was sad but all right. "I heard that you weren't close to your grandmother, but you were to Clarence. He was a nice man."

"He was nice. I didn't get to spend much time with him but we talked on the phone some. My dad, Chad Holt, isn't a nice man. He is not at all a good father either. It's been almost three months since he's picked me up when he's supposed to. Not that I care all that much. He makes me keep his house so that his girlfriend can laze about the house doing nothing. I don't want my mom to know, but I know that he's the one that hurt her this time—he broke her foot by stamping on it while she was down. Mom talks in her sleep sometimes. All the other times, he's hurt her too, I think." She thought about what her mom had told her. "Mom said that you were a wolf, a shifter. It's not that I don't believe her, but are you really?"

"Yes. My entire family are wolves. My older brother, Joel he's the leader of them all." She smiled, telling him that was so neat. "Yeah, I guess it is. You're human. But someone, I'm thinking my entire family has been giving you and your mother a little magic to keep you safe. Joel told me that your father is out to find your mother. Do you think he wants to hurt her again?"

"Yes. He does that when he's around, I guess. There is a reading of my grandpa's will tomorrow that we're going to go to. They had to put it off because your family wanted to be there for us. Dad is supposed to be there, too, and we're not sure how nice—though he never is—he'll be to us. I'm afraid if you want to know the truth. My mom, she's not getting around all that well, and she'll not be able to protect herself if he tries to hurt her. Your family told us that they'd be there, too, as her bodyguards, but I'm also afraid that they'll be hurt, too." Mr. Tate told her that he'd be dead if he tried anything. "That's what your dad told me. He's a funny man, isn't he?"

"He is. He's also a great dad for us all." Her heart hurt a little when she thought of the things that her dad had said to her when she visited him. "He won't get to you, Lynn. I swear to you that I'll protect you and your mom with my life. And if I can't do it because of me being so weak, my entire family will."

"Why?" He told her that was the right thing to do. "Sure, for people that are supposed to love us, but you don't know me from anyone else."

He started to speak, then stiffened. Standing up, ready to take on whatever he was afraid of, he told her to get under the bed and not to move. Doing just what he said, she was barely under the bed when the door opened and slammed hard against the other wall. It was her dad. And from the way he was cursing, he was spitting mad.

"Where are they?" Mr. Tate asked him who he was talking about. "Chalina and that daughter of hers. Where are they both hiding out? I was told that my daughter was here with her and I was going to bring her to the funeral. She messed up my plans, and I'm pissed off. She should know better than to go against me when I say something. Women. They're as stupid as the day is short."

"You'd have to be an idiot if someone didn't see that you're obviously pissed off. As for where they are, I haven't any idea." She saw her dad go to the bathroom and go inside. He started screaming for her, calling her *daughter*, the only thing that he ever called her when he came out. Lynn had to put her hand over her mouth so she'd not make a noise. *"He won't see you. I promise you that."*

She nearly screamed when she heard the voice in her head. She knew on some level that it was Mr. Tate, but she was no less afraid. Closing her eyes, she hoped that her mom would stay in her room until her dad was gone. But almost as soon as she thought that, the door opened, and she could see her mother's wheelchair making its way into the room.

Lynn didn't know what had happened. There was a loud scream, like a growl of some kind. Then her dad nearly fell over himself, trying to get past her mom and out the door. Lynn saw her wheelchair fall over, and she got out from under the bed to help her. Lynn was terrified that she'd be hurt badly if she couldn't at least try and get away.

"It's all right, little one. I've got you both." She didn't look at the woman who was talking to her. Her attention was on the large wolf that was where Mr. Tate had been. When he dropped to the bed, she went to him to help him get back into it. She was afraid that this was the something stupid that his dad had told him not to do. "Child, can you please look at me? I'd feel a good deal better if I could see that you're not injured."

"I'm not. Mr. Tate told me to get — is he going to be all right? He looks terrible." The woman told her to pet him. "Yeah, sure. While he has my hand for a snack. No thanks."

But she did scratch him behind the ears. He seemed to like that, so she sat on the bed and took his big paw into her hand. It occurred to her that when he'd—whatever it was called, he'd scared her dad off. Thinking of her mother then, Lynn got up to check on her.

"I'm sorry, Mom. I didn't mean to ignore you." She told her with laughter in her voice that she understood. She'd been distracted by the big wolf, too. "He is big, huh? I don't think that he should have done that. It's made him weaker, I think."

"I'm right here. You can both talk to me." She smiled when her mom whimpered when Mr. Tate spoke to them both in their heads. *"And you're right. I do feel weak, but I couldn't help but save the two of you. I just need to rest a bit more. Aurora, can you make sure that they're all right while I get something for pain?"*

"It would be my pleasure. However, I'm going to help the two of you along, Saul. That man isn't going to back off, and I don't want to have to worry about you getting harmed, too. Immortal means you live forever, but you can still hurt." All she did was touch her fingers to Mr. Tate's head, and he was himself again, and he looked better than he had since she'd been with him. Her mom, too. "There. You'll have the cast removed soon, my dear. We can't have you being hurt by that terrible man."

"Thank you, Aurora. You've no idea how much I appreciate that. More than I can explain to you." Mom was staring at her foot, and Lynn went to sit on the bed again with Mr. Tate. "Will you please stop calling me Mr. Tate? It's Saul. Even if you only do it in your head, I find I'm looking around for my grandda when you say that."

"You can read my mind, too? That's so awesome." She embarrassed herself when he laughed. Telling her that she was just what he needed, she didn't understand that and told him so. "Usually, it's only my mom that thinks I'm fun to be around. I don't think that either of us has had a good laugh in a long time."

"I'll have to take care of that." Aurora asked him if he needed anything else. "Yes, please. I would like to have the faeries finish my house. Please? I'm going to need it a good deal sooner than I thought." Mom finally looked at Saul when he said her name. "Where are the two of you staying right now?"

"A nice hotel. How did...all the pain is gone from my foot. I mean, even with medications, it still throbbed a bit. Now, it's all I can do not to get up and walk around. What happened that makes it feel like it's all healed up?" She looked at Aurora and then back at Saul. "Something is going on. You're talking, but it's not making any sense. You're the guy, right? Your brother said something about...it hits you all at one time. Mates. That's it. You think that I'm something to you. I'm sorry to tell you, Mr. Tate, but there is no way in hell that I can be what you need in a mate. Firstly...well, all of it that I'm human. Broke too. Not broke, but I have money in the bank, and that has to last me until I can work again. And if you tell me that I don't have to worry about money, then I'm going to smack the crap out of you. Everyone should — even people as rich as I've heard your family is, has to watch out for — I'm going to take a walk. Not a walk but a ride around to think. I have to think. And while I'm gone, you're going to get that mate stuff out of your head right now."

When her mom rolled herself out of the room, refusing help from Aurora, she looked at Saul when he started laughing. She told him that mom got upset when she was laughed at when she was mad, and that made him laugh all the harder. He told her that he had needed a good laugh.

"She's really going to smack you sillier if you keep that up. One thing about my mom you might want to know is that she's stubborn as a mule. And she doesn't suffer fools well. I'm not entirely sure what that means, but I don't think that you're going to be able to get around her on this mate thing." Saul asked her if she was all right with him seeing her mom. "I guess so. I mean, I don't know you all that well. I have a feeling that you're nothing like my dad. I'm betting that's why she doesn't want you to be her mate or whatever it is. She's afraid my dad will hurt you." She cocked her head at him when he laughed. "But you are a big wolf. Maybe you will be able to protect her. But if you hurt her, I don't care if you hurt her with your words. I'll never forgive you. No matter how long I live."

"I won't forgive myself either if I were to hurt either of you, Lynn." He looked at the door and then smiled. "My family is coming down the hall. I think that my sisters, my brothers' wives, are talking to your mom. That'll make her feel better, I hope."

"Don't count on it." Lynn was slightly afraid of the Tate men. Not that any of them had ever hurt her, but they were large, and now that she knew that they were all wolves, she was afraid of that, too. She wondered if they would protect her mom better than the police did. She asked Saul that while he was getting hugs from his family.

"Yes. We can smell when he's around quicker than the police can find him. By that, I mean that we can find him no matter where he is, even in a deep hole. Also, I don't mean to spring something else on you, but we have friends that are vampires as well as lions that can help us. If it comes to it, honey, we'll lay down our lives to keep you safe." He told her, too, that his brother and his brother's wife, Hanna, were the king and queen of all shifters. "They can and will call on an army if they need it. You and your mom will be protected well."

She didn't know what to believe but did leave them to their visit. Her mom was down the hall sitting on one of the couches when she found her. Her cast was gone, she noticed, and the other women were talking about the upcoming holiday. Halloween was a big deal for them, she supposed.

"Mom?" Her mom turned to her and smiled. Cuddling up next to her, the two of them listened to the women talking. When they asked her if she was going to help Saul decorate his house, she told them that she'd never been trick or treating before but did enjoy handing out candy. "I had to stay close so that my dad wouldn't hurt me. He used to do that all the time, but not much anymore."

"He's hurt you? When was the last time?" She told her mom that it had been the day before they'd left to come here. "What did he do to you? I'm going to murder him. I swear it. Show me, Lynn, what he did."

She'd forgotten that she shouldn't have said that, but she did get up and show her mom the marks on her back. Lynn wasn't able to see all the marks as it was hard to turn. But mom must have been able to see what he'd used too, a whip on her backside, because she could almost feel her anger as she tried to speak calmly to the other women.

"He hurt her. He's hurt her again." Mom

started crying, and it hurt her heart so bad that she didn't know what to do. Lynn hated that her dad was forever upsetting her mom, and she wanted to make sure that he didn't do it again. But she was only a kid.

It was the other women who comforted her. Telling her that they had her back and that he'd not do it again. "How do you think that's going to happen? He's forever sneaking around and beating the—he finds us at the grocery store. I finally just started ordering online because I think that the store employees called him when I was there."

"They did. He'd beat them if they didn't. I'm sorry about that." She asked Caitlynn how she knew that for sure. "Honey, we're going to have to set the two of you down and have a long talk about what we can do. It's mind-blowing. But it will keep the two of you safe. Of that, I can promise you."

When Saul came down the hall with his brothers and dad, she was happy to see that he looked better than he had before. Not only was he getting around on his own, but he seemed to have gotten some strength, too. Lynn had a feeling that it was because he'd found her mom, but she didn't know what was going on most of the time. Lynn decided that she was going to make a list of things that she wanted to know and see if she could get answers. Like, were there unicorns, too? Needing to have a quiet place to think, Lynn followed them all as they headed to the elevator.

Once they were in the limo that they'd been using to get around in, she sat in the corner and thought about everything that was going on. Not just with her dad and mom but with the people she was with. There was too much going on. Needing to chill, just for a few minutes, she asked Hanna, the one that had been left in the limo with her when they went to the hotel to get their things, if she could take a walk. Hanna said that she'd go with her.

"Of course you can. I'll go with you. Only to protect you, not to intrude. You won't even know that I'm around." Lynn wasn't sure how that was going to work, but she needed a minute. She and her mom were used to be just the two of them. It didn't look like that was going to happen again for a very long time.

Chapter 2

Chalina was sitting as far from Chad as she could manage and still be in the room with him. The reading of the will had been delayed twice now because of him, and she wanted it finished. Not that she expected to receive anything. She knew that she wasn't related to either of the Holts, but they'd been summoned, and that was why they were here. Today, it seemed Chad had been able to get his shit together and be there on time. More than likely, it was because the police had brought him in by order of the courts, but he was here, and it looked like they were going to be getting things cleared up once and for all. She glanced over at Saul, who was sitting between her and Chad, and was ever so happy for that. Lynn was sitting against the far wall where the credenza was.

Lynn seemed to be adjusting off and on to being here, she thought. The house and her having a huge bedroom was more than likely the reason that she stayed in her room so much. There were times when she would lash out, but those weren't that bad. While she'd not made a lot of friends yet, Lynn did seem to get along with the family. She did as well. They were all a great group of people.

"All right, everyone. We're here to read the will of Clarence Holt. Before we do that, however, I have a few things that I must clear up." Chad asked if it was going to delay things. "Not particularly. If I don't read this information, then I can't finish up with the will. Not my rules but those of the state. All right then. Chad. I have some questions here for you."

"I don't have time for this bullshit. Just give me my money, and I'll be on my way. I know how things work. My daddy died first, so everything went to mom. Even if she didn't have a will, it'll all come to me because I'm the last man standing up. Hand it over. I want it all in cash, too." Mr. Peabody said that he had to answer the questions. "Then fucking ask them, you idiot. I need to get moved into my mom's house. The police are keeping me from it on account of this shit not being done. Get on with it."

"All righty then. Did you know that Mr. Holt wasn't your biological father? Nor was the late James Holt your biological brother?" Chad said that everybody knew that. To move on. "When Mr. Holt married your mom, did he happen to adopt you as his own child? Now, be careful how you answer that young man. Did he officially adopt you?"

"Well, no. But he married my mom." Saul burst out laughing but turned it into a cough. "What the hell is funny to you? No, he didn't adopt me. I bet he would have, but it was never brought up. When they married up, I started using his last name. Mom said that it would make it easier on people — like I ever cared if they didn't have to remember Berkheimer and Holt in the same family."

"Ms. Chalina, when you were married to Mr. Berkhimer, did he ever suggest that you put his last name — Berkhimer on any kind of official paperwork?" Chalina said that she'd never seen any paperwork as he had raped her then took her before some police friends of his to get them married. "But you did sign your name to the certificate? You're officially married to Chad Holt, correct?"

"Yes. He even filled out the birth certificate of my daughter the same way. He snatched it from me when the nurse gave it to me and signed his name. Now that I think about it, he told the nurse how to spell the last name because she kept saying Help, not Holt." She looked at Chad and then at Mr. Peabody. "Is there something wrong?"

"Wrong? Good heavens, no. Everything is right as rain." Chad told Peabody that he was finished asking questions. To get on with it. "I'll get on with it as you say when I'm durn good and ready. Now you hush up and let me do my job, you mongrel. I'm the one asking questions. You sit your butt down right now before I have to find me a switch and use it on you. Now, as I was saying, I had some questions that I had to ask, and I did that. Now let me have a look."

Chalina had a few of her own but waited on Mr. Peabody. It was kind of fun, she had to admit, to have Chad pissed off because he wasn't getting his way. Not that she cared. Chalina had a lot of things to get taken care of as well, and if she didn't get them finished, she'd be just as all right with that, too. It was nice for a change in being a stay-at-home mom.

It wasn't as if she was lazing about the house. This morning, she'd gone over all the rooms they were using with a vacuum. Then she'd taken all the laundry down to the washer and dryer. She knew that having a set of machines on each floor was going to save her a lot of steps, and she didn't mind washing up the things. Even the kitchen area had a nice smaller set in a room where things could be tossed if they came into the house wet or dirty. Chalina thought that room was going to be very busy this coming spring through fall.

"All right then. As Estate Attorney for the State of Ohio, I declare this marriage certificate between Chad Birkhimer and Chalina Kennedy to be null and void. Also, the signed birth certificate for Lenette Kennedy to be—"

"Ha-ha, that means I'm not married to you, Chalina. That's the best news that I've heard all damned day. No more child—does she have to pay back all the child support to me?" Chalina told him that he'd never paid her a dime. "Well then, maybe you should be paying me something to not being married to you no more. Hot damn, I'm one happy feller. You can depend on that. What do you think of that, Daughter? I'm not your daddy anymore. That's the best news I've—" Chad paused in his excitement. "Not that I care, but why come does she not have to be my ex-anything from now on. Nor is that my kid. What do you care?" Chad was still laughing like he'd won the big prize. Chalina didn't care that she'd never been married to Chad, but it was her daughter she was thinking about. "You gonna tell me, or do I gotten beat it out of you, Mr. Peabody?"

"Mr. Berkheimer, you falsified state records. Not just once but two times when it comes to this little family. And you should have been paying for child care for your daughter anyway. You acknowledged her. Even though you did it incorrectly, she is still your biological daughter. Just because you were a fool and didn't know enough to put your right name on paperwork doesn't mean that Ms. Kennedy here should suffer, do you think?"

"I don't care what anyone says, she'd not my kid, and I'm not paying her shit. Not now, not fucking ever. When can I get my money? I know that old Holt had a lot of insurance for him and my mom. You just tell me how much I'm going to get today, and I'll be happier than a pig in a mud bath to wait around for the rest. Not too long, though. I still got shit I have to do." He looked over at her. "I guess that means that I never beat you up either while we weren't married. This is the funniest thing in the world, don't you think?"

"What about my daughter? Will we have to file another certificate for her birth?" Chad said it didn't matter none to him, he wasn't signing shit. "I'm not talking to you, you overgrown shit. I'm talking about my daughter."

"She'll be a Kennedy. Even if Mr. Birkhimer were to sign a second certificate, Ms. Kennedy, she would still be a Kennedy. Thankfully, you weren't married to Mr. Birkhimer. If you will allow me a few moments here, I'll explain this to you." She couldn't help but smile back at Saul when he looked at her. "I swear, honey, this is going to turn out for the best."

"I should hope so." Saul took her hand into his and held it. He reached for Lynn's, too, but instead of taking his hand, she jerked away from him. While she didn't get what was going on, Lynn did eventually take his much larger one into her own. "We'll be all right. I don't know why we were called here if it was just to humiliate us by you not having a father named on your birth certificate."

"Mr. Berkheimer, you may leave. The questions that you've answered for me have cleared a great many things up. And there is no other reason for you to stay. You can get on with the things that you claimed you had to do today." Chalina thought for sure she'd missed something while musing about her daughter, but apparently, Chad didn't understand either. He asked about his money. "There is a stipulation in Mr. Holt's will that states that you were not his son, so there is no obligation for him to leave you anything in his will. You did a good job of verifying his statement that you are not in any relation to him whatsoever. You may leave on your own, or I'll have you escorted out by the police. You have nothing to gain by fighting me on this."

"But it's my money. My mom, she would have left it to me if she'd gotten off her ass and made out a will. I can't be punished for her stupidity. It's not right." Chalina looked at the door when it opened, and several officers came in with their hands on their guns. "This is stupid. Who gets his money? That kid there isn't his granddaughter either if I'm not his son. Don't tell me that he's done and went to leave it to that kid. I'll make sure she's not able to collect on shit if she's the one getting it all."

"Officers, please toss this man out of this building." Chalina watched as they jerked Chad up from his chair and handcuffed him. She wasn't sure what was going to happen to him, but she thought that if anyone were to even get a stain on their clothing, Chad would be shot so full of holes that they'd not have enough to bury him left over. Once he was gone, bitching and screaming about how it was his money, they all turned to Peabody. "The will is pretty straightforward from now on. He changed his will on the day that Lynn was born. While he did know that she wasn't his granddaughter, he was thrilled beyond words that she would call him grandpa. Mr. Holt led a very sad life after he was married. As most people can attest to, I believe."

"He left it all to Lynn? I'm not sure how much there is, but I'm positive that it can't be right."

Lynn told her to hush up. "Sorry, that didn't come out right. What I mean is, didn't he have, I don't know, some cousins or something?"

"Gee, thanks, Mom. You think that I'm not good enough for someone to leave me something in their will." Saul said she hadn't meant that. "I know my mom better than you do, I think."

"Lynn, there is no reason for you to speak to him like that." She asked why he was even there in the first place. "What is wrong with you? He's here because I asked him to be. Let's let Mr. Peabody speak, and then we'll go home and talk. Your attitude is getting out of control."

"Whatever." There had been times over the last several days with her daughter that she had wanted to smack her. But so far, she'd not. Not that she didn't deserve it, but her mouth was going to bite off more than she could chew if she kept it up.

"To my darling granddaughter, Lynette Kennedy — I should point out here that Mr. Holt was aware of the things that happened between you and Mr. Birkhimer. He also knew, since her birth, that Chad had filled out his paperwork incorrectly when getting married as well as her birth." She asked why he'd not said anything. "He knew that soon enough that someone would figure it out. However, he left me a note in the packet of the will that had me checking in on things. Mr. Holt, believe it or not, was a good attorney and had been planning for this day for a really long time. Anyway, I leave Lynette Kennedy the house that I shared with her biological grandmother. She hated the house and was never one to hold back on it when she was upset about things. But it's all yours, including the contents. I do hope that you can bring laughter to the walls again, as my parents lived in that house when I was born."

"I have my own house? How flipping cool is that?" She noticed that Saul started to speak, but she only had to put her hand on his leg for him to wait. "I'm going to use it for the rest of my life."

"There is also my estate that Lynette will get half of. The other half will go to Ms. Chalina Kennedy. It will never make up for the years of abuse that you endured, but I do hope that this money does some good for you. I want to point out that as of this morning, each of you will get one point one million dollars. I'll read the rest now. This doesn't include the insurance that I've had on myself and my wife. You might say that I had an inkling that Mabel wasn't going to end up dying of old age. There is a double of both policies if we're murdered. If you're hearing this, it means that I'm gone, and hopefully, so is Mabel. As for the insurance, it's a great deal of money. I would like you to contact the Tates foundation and make sure that they can use it for something that Mabel would have hated. A scholarship comes to mind."

Both she and Saul laughed. When looking over at Lynn, she could tell that she was thinking about the money. Lynn wasn't going to allow her to spend her money on stupid things, but she would, however, allow her to have a nice spending spree when things settled down. She had no idea what she was going to do with her part of the money, but she was sure that it would be something fun. Maybe she'd pay for them to have a lovely vacation. One that would require them to have a passport. Yes, she thought, the perfect thing to do with the money.

The money that was coming to them was in several certified checks. A bank would have trouble giving out two million dollars if they wished for cash, so each check was for a smaller amount to be cashed out. But for now, she was going to talk to

Saul about investing for the two of them. It would be a shame for them to get to the end of their lives and not have a thing to show for it. Chalina put both thick envelopes in her purse.

"I can hold onto my own money, Mom. I know that I can't spend any of it right now." She said she was going to hold onto it. "No, you're going to hand it to me now. It's all mine, and I don't want you to have it. Please?"

"Putting a *please* at the end of a demand doesn't make it any less demanding, Lynn. You can have a portion of it when we get home. End of discussion, Lynn." She huffed all the way to the car. Chalina didn't have to remind Saul that ignoring her was the best way of dealing with a kid. "I thought we'd get some dinner with our new status as millionaires."

"So long as you don't spend any of my money." She heard her daughter but again, chose to ignore her. "I'd like to go and get a steak dinner. With pie. Grandpa Holt loved pie."

She knew that about the older man. Any kind of pie, he was happy to have it. As they were being driven to Columbus to have a good dinner, the three of them talked about anything but the money. Lynn seemed to have gotten a good deal more polite as well, especially to her.

When they were finished with their meals, stuffed beyond anything she'd ever been before, they took a walk about just so they'd not be uncomfortable when riding back to their home.

"Chad has been arrested." Both she and Lynn asked him at the same time what he'd done now. "He accosted Mr. Peabody when he came out of his offices tonight. The older gentleman is in the hospital, but he says that he'd fine. My brothers don't think he is. Chad was still standing there over him with a bat in his hands when the police arrived. Also, there is a warrant out for his arrest about some unpaid tickets from where he lived."

"How do you know that?" Saul told Lynn that his brothers knew, so they told him so we'd not worry when we got home. "I don't worry about my dad. He'll have to be nicer to me now that I have lots of money."

Lynn skipped ahead of them to the car. She wasn't nasty about what she said to them, but it worried Chalina no less. Chalina asked Saul what he thought of how she was acting.

"I don't know. I didn't know her all that well

when we first met, so this seems normal to me. I have caught her being rude to one of my brothers a couple of times, but they shut that down quickly. My dad, too. Again, he doesn't mind telling her to behave herself. I hope that's all right?" Chalina said that it was. She'd not have it any other way. "I think, and I don't know, she might be lashing out because her entire life has changed in the last few months. Not only does she have a stepfather, almost, anyway, but she's moved and lost her grandda and grandma. She didn't have a good relationship with Mabel, but she knew her."

"You're more likely right on that. This—I'm going to call it what it is. Being a bitch is going to stop. I wouldn't tolerate it from anyone else, especially my own daughter. Thank you." They were in the limo and on their way home when Saul told her through their link that Mr. Peabody had suffered a stroke and had died. *"Oh no. He was such a nice man, too."*

"Why does Saul have to sit next to you all the time, Mom?" Saul asked Lynn if she wanted him to sit with her. "No. I don't think that I even like you anymore. You're always hogging my mom all the time. Why don't you go to work or something?

Why do you have to be with us all the time? It's not right."

"This is the first time that I've sat next to your mom in days, if you don't count the attorney's office." Saul tried to tease Lynn into a better mood, but it didn't seem to be working. "Come on, Lynn, I love your mother. I love you, too. If you'd allow it anyway."

"I have a father, thank you very much." She could tell that hurt Saul. Before she could react and discipline Lynn, Saul spoke. His voice was smooth as silk, soft too, but there was a hardness to it that frightened her a little.

"You do. And such a stellar man, too. I wasn't going to tell you until we were home, but your wonderful dad murdered Mr. Peabody. He was a federal employee, and that will cost him a lot of years behind bars." She asked him if he'd get him out. Or could she use her own money to bail him out. "There will be no bail set for him. Until his trial, he'll be in the local jail. Sorry, you can't be his knight in shining armor this round." He looked at her and told her he was sorry. That he'd been petty.

"No, you weren't. You were hurt, and I don't

blame you. I'm going to have a long talk with her when we get home. Then I might end up beating her butt. Your dad said that was the way that he dealt with you boys." He said that his dad hadn't ever hit them. *"He told me that, too. He said you six were the very best and that he was proud to be your father."*

The rest of the ride was done in silence. Not even when Lynn fell asleep did she or Saul speak. Thinking about the way that Lynn was acting hurt her. She knew that she had hurt Saul, too. It was as if she were trying to pull them apart. Why would she do that, Chalina wondered. They had such a good life right now.

~*~

Saul was avoiding the women in his house. Mostly Lynn. But when the younger one was around, Chalina would get mad and loud, and then they'd go all over the house screaming at one another.

"Is it safe?" Saul shook his head at this dad and mouthed that he'd follow him outside. Once they were on the front porch, they sat in the rockers and didn't speak for several moments. He could still hear them arguing in the house. "What's going on with the two of them all of a sudden? They're forever bickering."

"If I knew, I'd fix it. I try my best to stay out of the way. Lynn seems to hate me most of all. And if I even dare to sit next to her mother for any reason, she leaps at me with her verbal abuse, and I have to walk away. I've never felt so helpless in my entire life." Dad told him that Lynn had gotten snippy with him a couple of days ago. Telling him that she wasn't going to be putting up with him for much longer. "What did she mean by that? She's not threatening you, is she?"

"No. Goodness gracious, no. She followed her threat up with her moving into her own house and not having anything to do with the rest of us, Tates. You know how she is. She's going to take her money and her house, and it's going to be all hers. I wish she'd move into that dab blame house and leave us all alone. You don't know how many times I've wanted to snatch her up and put her in it. I'd even be willing to buy her groceries and set them by the steps if she'd go there. I never thought that I'd be this sick of a kid in my life." Saul told his dad that he was feeling the same thing. Every day was an uphill battle.

"Chalina is getting the worst of it. Every time they're out, and there are people about, Lynn does the same thing. My house. My money. You'd think that she was the only one that had any, and she's not sharing." Saul looked out over the yard and then back at his dad. "Mom would have beaten us if we'd acted like that. Then she would have beaten us again because she had to beat us."

"She sure would have. Then she'd of cried for a month cause you made her do it." They both laughed. "I don't know what you're going to do, Saul. But we can't even get together now with her bickering all the time. I don't want to be around her. How sad is that when a man don't want to be around his own—" Dad looked around then back at him and whispered 'granddaughter.' "She surely will throw a fit if she hears me calling her that out loud. She tells anyone around that she has her own daddy and that he's going to be nicer to them now that there is her money in the house. I don't know why she'd think that is going to fly, but I've been around a tad bit longer than she has, and nobody ever changes for the good where money is involved."

"No. You're right about that. But I do like your idea about her going to the house. However, I believe she thinks that her mom is going to—

you don't think she will, do you, Dad? Leave me because of her daughter? Christ, I don't know what I'd do if she did that to me. I'd just want to curl up in a ball and stop breathing."

"It won't come to that, son. Something is going to give, and it's not going to be you or her momma. Wait and see. She's going to tire of all this going on around her where people are avoiding her like she's diseased or something. Mark my words. It's going to come back and haunt her. See that it does." Saul wasn't so sure. He'd heard them fighting, and it was vicious and hurtful. The things that she would say to her mom were like a dagger to his heart each time she opened her mouth. "I hear her coming."

The door to the front porch flew open, and there stood Lynn. Her cheeks were bright pink, and her hair was falling out of the messy like bun she'd had it in this morning. There were stains on her shirt that he didn't want to think about, as well as little flecks of something on her face.

"Where did she go?" Saul turned his face away from her and reached out to Chalina. She told him that she needed a break and was going to lunch with the women. "Did you hear me ask you a question? Where is my mother? Did you lock her away from me again?"

"Again?" He told his dad that he would explain that later. Lynn told his dad her version of what happened. "I doubt very much that Saul shackled your mother up and strung her from the rafters, young lady. Why don't you try telling me the truth."

"Like I care if you have the truth. All you people do is take my mom away from me so that I can't be with her. We've been together all this time without your interference and help and got along just fine. I don't know why you won't just leave us alone and let us live out our lives in my house. We have enough money to take care of ourselves." She put her hands on her hips and glared at him. "Where is my money, anyway? You said you were going to give it to me when you cashed out the checks. I want it today. No more lying to me about it. You bring it to me today, or I'm going to call the police on you. You're keeping me from my mom and —"

"Fine." She leapt back from him when he stood up. He didn't feel good about that, scaring her. He wanted them to be a happy family. But at the rate they were going now, it would be forever for them to be even on friendly terms. "I'll take it to your house. That way, it doesn't have to be sullied up at all with my house."

He walked off the porch, forgetting about his dad. Getting into his car, he was just about to slam it in reverse when the other door opened. Dad asked him if he should be driving.

"No. But I will let you once I'm out of sight of her. I just need to show her…Dad, I don't know what I want to show her, but I need this right now." He barely got to the end of the drive without the shakes setting in.

He'd never been this mad before. Not ever that he could think of. Once he was calm enough to get out of his truck without ripping the door off, he calmly—he had to keep telling himself that he needed to remain calm—got out of the truck, leaned against the hood of it, and closed his eyes.

"Son?" He told his dad that he'd be all right in a moment. "I don't know. You don't look so good. Want me to go and get Chalina?"

"She's going to hang out with the women at Joel's home. He's on a business trip, remember?" Dad said that he did. "Lucky him." Saul looked at his dad. "I don't know what to do, Dad. Not a single thought to my head comes to mind in making her behave. I don't care that she doesn't…well, I do care, but the way she treats Chalina breaks me in half."

"I don't know what to tell you, son. I've never in all my years run into something like this. She wasn't like that when they first came here." Saul said that she'd not been. He did tell his dad that she'd had a lot going on when she came here. "Don't make excuses for her. This is beyond rude. Someone's going to take exception to her and hurt her bad. The way that she talks about her dad, I'm worried she's going to try and cozy up to him, and he's going to take her life."

"That's what worries me, too." Dad told him to let her see him. "You mean to take her to the jail? I can't do that."

"Why not?" He started to say that she wasn't his daughter, but it wasn't that. He'd never forgive himself is something happened to her. "That might be just what she needs. A good dose of reality.

He didn't want to bother Chalina with it right now. She was hopefully relaxing, and that's what she would need to bring around her daughter this morning. As his dad drove him into town, he had to think about how he was going to get the cash for Lynn. Then he thought fuck it—she'd get what he could get and then cash the rest out the way he'd have to do. He only hoped that she didn't spend it all in one day.

Chapter 3

Chad didn't want to have a visitor. He wanted the fuck out of here so that he could get going on his plans to get his money. While he didn't know which one of the others had it, he knew that he'd not have any trouble killing off them both to get at it. There wasn't no reason for him to have to do without when his momma should have been better at taking care of him in her after life.

"Stupid woman. For all her planning, she surely did fuck up when it came to me having an easy life." He heard the door at the end of the hallway open and then close. Using the mirrors that were up and down the long hall, he could see that it was some kid and an officer. If they thought that he was going to be babysitting around here, they were dumber than Chalina was in not giving him a son when he'd told her to. Then he saw who it was. "What do you want? Better yet, tell me who got all the money, and I might let you have a bit of it."

"I got half, and my mom got the other half. But the stupid tax people, they took a lot of it. That's what I came here to talk to you about. My money." He asked her how it was her money. "Because Grandpa Holt left it to me. Well, half, like I said. I got one point one million dollars before the taxes were taken out."

"How much you got left? I'm telling you right now, you had better not have spent it all already. I'll beat you to death." One of the officers brought down a chair and opened it up for Daughter. They sure were nice to her, and he had a thought that they were being paid to be nice to her. "You making promises with my money, Daughter? If you are, you'd better know that I'm not going to be bailing you out for shit. That money should have come to me and not nobody else."

"He left it to me, and I'm going to make a deal with you about it. That's why I'm here today. To talk to you about being nice to me and my mom." He asked her what she was talking about.

"I'll give you some of my money if you were to be nice to mom and me and not beat us up anymore. No more hurting us when you see us. You can even live in my house, the one that Grandpa Holt gave me, if you behave yourself. With you being there, that Tate man won't be hanging around mom all the time. You can scare him away."

"Scare him away, huh. What? You don't like your momma being with one of them shifter people? Or is it the rich people you don't like none? He's got a powerful bit of money, that family does." She asked him if he'd heard her tell him that she had money, too. "Yeah? You got what? I'd say only about half that million that you were supposed to get. Ain't that about right? He's got about a hundred times that, I hear."

"Nobody has that much money." He assured her that he did. That the Tates were worth billions. "No way. If he does, he sure doesn't flash it around, does he? What would a person...he could buy whatever he wanted and have money left over too."

"Pretty much." She shook her head at him and said that she didn't believe he had crap. "Whatever you say. So you want me to live with you and your momma in that house that my mom had, and I'm not allowed to hit on you or her. Is that about right?"

"Yes. No stealing either. I'll give you some money that you can use when you want it. I don't know how much it'll be. They keep telling me that you won't have a bail set on account of you killing that lawyer. Why did you go and kill him anyway?" He told her that it wasn't any of her business, and then he told her why he'd done it. "He'd already given me and my mom the money. You killing him didn't help you any, now did it? You'll have to not do that anymore, either. I only got so much money to use to bail you out all the time."

He didn't care for her pointing out things that he'd done wrong. She was reminding him too much of his mother, and she was forever pointing out things that he'd not done the way he should have. Even things that she'd told him to do were wrong in her eyes. Like raping Chalina. He'd given her a grandbaby, didn't he?

Momma had never liked his choice of women. Even when he was just a kiddy, and he'd be sweet on some little girl at school. The first thing she did was point out to him all her flaws, and then she'd tell him what sort of babies she'd have. She was forever telling him that the women, no matter the age, were defective around this town. Even little babies — he knew that she pinched them hard on the legs to make them scream when she was around them. His momma, she didn't suffer fools well. Not that he understood that any more than when she told him that women were only out for one thing. He thought it'd been sex, which he didn't understand either. He liked sex well enough, and he wasn't defective. Momma's logic was sometimes —

"Are you listening to me?" He hadn't been and told her that. "Then why am I telling you the rules if you're not going to be able to remember them. There are a lot of them, you know. Mostly, it's the not beating us up ones, but you also gotta help around the house and stuff."

"I ain't doing no women's work. You can just cross that off your list right now." She rolled her eyes at him, and that made him nearly blind with anger. "You keep spouting off that smart mouth of yours, and you're going to be picking up your face on the other side of the room."

"What? I think you just made that up. How would I pick my face up on...you know what, I don't care. We're going to go over the rules again. You'd better be paying attention. I have to be going home soon, and I don't want to be late getting there." He asked her what she had to do at home. "Nothing. But I don't want to be outside after dark. I'm not afraid of the dark, but I don't want to be out in it either."

He allowed her to prattle on for a bit more, and then his dinner tray was brought to him. Chad had a system for eating his meals. He wanted it quiet and no one bothering his plate either. Thinking on the word system, he knew that was wrong. Someone had told him once that he didn't have a system but a routine. Whatever, he wasn't going to allow the brat to talk to him, or he supposed at him while he was eating. It would give him the most god-awful heartburn in the world.

"You have to keep your trap shut while I'm eating." She told him that she could go over the rules while he ate so he didn't need to speak. "No. Shut up. I don't like it when you're jabbering all the time while I'm trying to enjoy my meal. Just keep your mouth shut while I eat, or I'll shut it for you."

"You say the dumbest things." He reached out and grabbed the back of her head. He was surprised that she was even that close. Looking at the look of shock on her face gave him a little tickle, but slamming her head into the bars gave him a thrill that he was going to enjoy for days on end. Turning his back to her bleeding on the floor, he opened up his tray lids and saw that he was having a thick sammich.

Normally, he didn't like sammiches all that much. He was more of a meat person. Just meat, too. None of that other crap that people put on them. If he wanted lettuce or to-mater with his food, he'd have a salad. And there wasn't any way that he was going to be eating one of them suckers if he didn't have to. But this was a good one. A lot of roast beef and mayo to make it perfectly sloppy.

After he finished off his sammich, he started on his chips. That was something that he could eat with every meal. A big bag of salty chips washed down with a soda pop. He only had a little bitty one today, but that was all right. They were salty enough that he didn't mind so much.

They used to bring him an apple or a pear.

Neither one of them he liked, so they gave him a couple of 'nanners. They weren't too brown or anything, and he just loved the way that they could make a room smell good with their 'nanner smells everywhere. As he was finishing off the last bite of the last of his food, he heard the door open up and close.

"What the hell did you do?" He had forgotten about Daughter. She was still leaning into the bars with her face all smashed up. There was a lot of blood, too, but none of it had gotten on him, so he was happy for that. The officer asked him why he didn't call for help when she was hurt. "I'm going to have to call her parents and an ambulance, Chad. What did you do that for?"

"She wouldn't shut up when I told her to. And I'm her parent. Or so I've been told. Anyhow, she's quiet now, and I didn't get anything on my clothing. I only just banged her the one time. It's not my fault. She just goes on and on about shit." He was told to step back to the wall, and he did. "You're making a big fuss about nothing. I was able to eat without any trouble after I quieted her down."

"I don't care about you, you brainless fuck.

You could have killed her." Chad didn't see what the big deal was. He'd managed to not just eat his lunch without any heartburn, and he'd not gotten a single spot of blood on his clothing either.

He had to stand against the far wall even after the ambulance arrived. The medics were talking like it was a big deal that she was hurt on both sides of her head. He'd not thought of how small her head was and how it wouldn't fit through the bars. She'd have twin sores when they fixed her up. Once they were finished working on her, he asked if he could take a nap now. He'd been standing for far too long.

"No. You'll stand there until I say differently." Chad didn't know why everyone was up in arms about the kid. It wasn't like she was going to have anyone mourn over her if she was to keel over or something. She was only a girl, for Christ's sake.

He saw Chalina and that man of hers when he was given permission to sit down on the floor. Chad didn't much care for the way they were screaming at him but he let them go on. They should have been thanking him for showing her what happens if you didn't shut up when you were told. He'd had to learn that lesson the hard way himself when he'd been a kid.

"You son of a bitch, I'm going to kill you." He asked the man what he was talking about. "You could have killed her with your actions. She's just a little girl. Why would you hurt her like that?"

"Like I said, she wouldn't shut her mouth. Christ, oh mighty, it's bad enough that she thinks I'm going to be following her rules about her money and house. She actually thinks that I'm going to just say okay, I won't hit you and your momma anymore so long as you give me the money that should have been mine in the first place." He stood up and nearly stepped toward the big man when the officer next to him drew his gun. "You're all brave when you got someone there that has a pistol, aren't you, jack turd. You make sure she brings me that money the next time that she comes here to visit me. And you make sure she knows that I make the rules on account of me being her daddy. I'll beat her more if she tries that shit again. Stupid female."

If he was honest with himself, which really he never was honest with other people, there was no reason for him to be honest with himself, but he was a little afraid of the big man. He'd heard that they were all them shifter people, the kind that turned into wolves or some kind of dog. Staying back as far as he could from the bars, he kept an eye on the man while he paced back and forth in front of the bars like he'd seen animals do when they were caged up.

"Why? Why did you hurt her?" He told Chalina that he wasn't going to explain it to nobody else. "She's just a little girl, and you…you could have crushed her skull. She might even have brain damage."

"I already think she had that. All she talks about is rules and money. I'll live with the two of you, but I'll be knocking you around—" He looked at the man. "Did you just growl at me? You ain't to do that again, you hear me? It scares me a bit, and I don't care for you anyway. It wasn't my idea that I live with them but that daughter. She wants me to scare you away. I'm thinking she might have it all wrong, but that's what she said to me. Get on away from me while I talk to Chalina."

"I'm pressing charges. Attempted murder of a minor." Chad asked Chalina why she'd do something like that. "You nearly killed her. I'm going to see you in hell before you're ever going to see the light of day again."

Just like a woman, he thought. Making things a lot bigger and worse than they really were. It wasn't that bad. Just a couple of bumps on her head. Stupid kid. It was her fault anyways. Of course, he'd not seen her face, but he'd only hit her there the one time. That's not bad enough to be called attempted murder or shit like that.

~*~

Saul knew the exact moment when Lynn woke up. Putting his hand on her shoulder, he told her that she was safe. When she turned in his direction, he adjusted himself in the seat so that he could lean in closer to her to speak to her. The doctor told him that using their link might hurt her head too bad to do right away.

"Where is my mom? Is she all right?" He told her that she was sleeping in the chair beside her. "He hurt me. He hurt me bad, didn't he?"

"He did. I'm not going to tell you what happened. The staff thinks it would be better and easier on you to remember on your own." Lynn raised her hand up, and he put his near enough that she could take it if she wanted. She latched onto his hand tightly. "I have some things to tell you. Things that happened when you were hurt."

"I feel weird. Like my skin is crawling all over me." Saul told her that she'd been changed into a wolf. She was quiet for a few minutes when she told him that her father had hit her head on the bars. "He just reached out and slammed my head on them. I don't remember what happened after that. You said that I'm a wolf now?"

"Yes." He waited to see if she would say more. Then she asked him if she had been very hurt. "You were brain-dead when you were brought here. Without mine and some other people giving you a part of themselves, you would have been in a vegetative state for the rest of your life. You're very lucky that we were on our way to the police station, or you wouldn't have survived."

"I'm immortal, though." He said that she still would have had severe brain damage. "So I would have been this...I don't know what it's called forever had you not saved me. Is that right?"

"Yes, it's right." She squeezed. "There is something else, isn't there? Something that you're working up to. Other than the wolf thing."

"You had a brain tumor that was pressing

on your brain and causing your emotions to be out of whack. When Chad hit your head on the bars, as you remember, he exposed a part of your brain where the tumor was. It was growing at a fast rate, the doctor told us, and if you'd not been hurt, it would have taken over the part of your brain that deals with emotions completely. It would have required that you be locked away, it would have caused you to have no emotions at all, and that would have been dangerous for anyone you came in contact with."

"I don't understand." He tried explaining it to her so that she'd understand. He didn't dumb it down so much as make several comparisons using his hands and hers to show her on his head where it was. "You're saying that I would have gotten meaner and meaner until I killed everyone."

"That's right. The issue is that since you are immortal, eventually, you would have had to be put to death by having your head removed. That is the only way that you can truly be killed." She held his hand, and he hurt for her. "There's more if you're ready for it."

"No. Not yet. I was just...I was mean to everyone. I remember telling my mom that I hated her. And you." He said that it wasn't her but the tumor. "Still, I think I have a lot to make up for, I think. Do you think that everyone will forgive me?"

"Everyone already has." When Calina moved closer to the bed after speaking, Saul expected Lynn to let go of his hand and hold onto her mother. But she held onto them both. "I don't want you to think about what you did when you were ill, Lynn. I'm just so glad that you're going to get better now. I feel horrible for not having you tested sooner."

"Don't say that. Please. I...just love me. Please? I'm so sorry that I hurt you. I know that I did, and I hate myself for that."

Saul said that he was going to contact his family and kissed the back of Lynn's hand when he let her go. But when she took his hand again, he felt his eyes fill with tears. After all that they'd been through, it looked like Lynn was going to be all right.

When the nurse came in to take her blood pressure, he did step out. Saul leaned against the wall, letting his own emotions get the better of him. While standing there, he reached out to his family and told them that not only was Lynn awake but that she was talking with her mom. He even told them how she'd taken his hand and held onto it.

"Does she know everything?" Saul told his dad that she didn't. Just that she was a wolf and that she'd had a brain tumor that had nearly cost her her life. *"I don't envy you having to tell her everything. It's going to be hard on her. Poor little...I can't believe that we didn't think that something was wrong with her after her being such a sweet little thing when she arrived."*

"The doctor told us that she was lucky in that we all were there for her." Aurora had given her the most magic, but that's not to say she didn't get a great deal from the other beings in the family. *"I don't want to think about what would have happened had we not been there. It hurts me in ways...I was ready to write her off and get on with my life. I feel so guilty."*

"I think we were all about to do the same thing, son. You have her back again, and I'd do everything in my power to forget that she'd been so close to...well, I can't talk about it either. Just breaks my heart that she had to suffer through all that on her own." He thanked his dad. "No reason for that. She's all right now, so we have to focus on the future instead of the past. We all do. And when she's well enough for us to come see her, we'll make sure she knows it too."

He entered the room just as the nurse was removing some of the bandages. He needed to talk to Lynn first. He'd promised Chalina that he'd be the one that broke the news about her eye site to her. Losing an eye was going to be difficult for her, but also being blind in the other one was going to be hard for all of them to get over.

"I spoke to her." Nodding, he sat down when Chalina spoke to him as the nurse talked about what she was doing to her each step of the way. "I don't know that it's hit her yet what I said, but she knows that she's going to be blind."

"I'm sorry, honey." She kissed him on the back of his hand when she said it was all right. "Are you going to be okay, Lynn? Is there anything that I can do for you? I want you to know that I love you with all my heart."

"I love you too." She was crying. He could hear it in her voice. "I thought that he'd change, you know? That he'd want to be a good dad to me. Is he still in jail? I hope he rots there."

"He will." He thought about what Hudson

had told him a couple of nights ago. That he'd fix it so that Chad was never heard from again. It was something he'd done for the family before, taken out someone that needed to just be gone. Now, here they were again, just wanting to move on with their lives, and some idiot bastard was mucking up the works.

Lynn fell asleep when the pain got to be too much for her and was given pain medication. With the bandages off her face, she looked ten times worse than he remembered from the jail. Christ, every time he looked at her, he wanted to kill Chad himself. Tear him apart into small pieces before he was dead.

From her forehead to her chin on the left side of her face was swollen so badly that it looked as if she not only didn't have an eye there but that her nose and lips were gone as well. The colors of the bruising was sickening to him. He couldn't imagine the pain she must be in on just that side of her face.

Her right side was bruised, too. The stitches from the top of her head to her throat were horrific. A part of her ear had been temporarily removed so they could get to the tumor to have it taken out.

When it was put back, because of the swelling, it looked like she'd been given an ear that was much too large for her little girl's face.

It was a wonder to him that she could even speak. She looked like she'd been beaten up and put back together from other parts of her body. The damage done to her small face was extensive, and the doctor told them that she was going to need more surgery in the future to make sure that she didn't have such terrible scarring. All in all, she had over four thousand stitches in her face and head. But she was alive and well, and he knew that, in the end, that was more important than her having a few scars.

He did wonder if when she was able to shift, if they'd go away on their own, but no one had an answer for him. There was just too much damage to know right now. Joel seemed to be looking into every book he could find to have good news for Lynn. Everyone was cheering for his little girl, and he couldn't have been happier than he was at the moment.

Once Calina was settled into the chair again, he told her that he'd go and get them something to eat. It was Hudson who brought them dinner.

It wasn't anything that he would have gotten himself. And not have it come back to them still steaming hot.

Steak and baked potatoes were perfectly done, and the rolls, still hot from the oven, took to the butter like they were meant for one another. Drinking the champagne that he had also brought them, Saul felt better than he had in a while. He supposed it had a lot to do with having a good meal with a beautiful woman.

Not that he thought things would be any kind of normal for a while, but he did believe that once they got Lynn home, there would be good things to celebrate. Then, he was going to marry Chalina if she would allow him to do that and adopt Lynn. He hoped that she'd be all right with that now that she was getting healthy.

Chapter 4

Chad was ready for this court shit to be finished with. He'd demanded to see Chalina and that daughter of his but no one was cooperating. That kid owed him some money, and he was going to see to it that she handed it over to him. And there wasn't going to be any more of him having to be nice to get it, either. She was going to hand it over without any fuss, or he'd have to do a little more damage on that face of hers.

He really hadn't any idea what he'd done to her. When she'd been laid out at the other side of his cell, he'd only seen a lot of blood. He figured that with blood, there had to be some damage. Whatever it was, she was going to get more than that if she didn't come through with the cash. Chalina too. It was rightfully his, damn it.

"Mr. Berkhimer? It's time for you to get cleaned up for court in an hour." He told the man that he didn't need to get nothing of the sort as he wasn't going to be there all that long. "You can do it my way, or you can do it the hard way. Up to you. I have to tell you that I'm more than willing to do it the hard way to you, the way you hurt that little girl of yours."

"Here we go again. I suppose you've never beat your kids? Sometimes they just need someone to smack their asses. My mom certainly did it when I needed it." When he didn't, too, but that wasn't going to happen again. The old bitty was dead. "Just get over yourselves. She got what she needed."

"She's blind. Do you think she deserved that? How do you think she's going to go through life now, knowing that her own father smashed in her face and made it so she can't see anymore. You fucking bastard. You're just lucky that I wasn't able to let Saul in there with you when he got here. We'd be cleaning up your dead body for years. And you know what? I'd do it with a smile on my face." Chad asked him if he was lying to him. To get a rise out of him today. "Why should I care if you get pissy. That little girl can't see anymore. Blind because of what you did to her. Didn't it occur to you that smashing her smaller head up against steel bars might do a bit of damage to her face? Or even kill her? If not for the medics, they said that she'd be dead now. So don't go spouting off to people that you only hit her a little because she needed it. No one needs to be hurt like that. Especially when it's your own child."

Chad must have been thinking too hard when he found himself in the shower stall with other inmates. The jail was a little crowded today, he noticed, and he didn't like to share, especially not the shower. Shady things happened in the showers on account of there being no cameras.

He was willing to overlook it this one time because he had court today just as he was getting under the hot spray. When someone hit him from behind, and he hit his head on the concrete wall, he had a moment of fear. Seeing stars, he was still staggering around when his legs were knocked out from under him, and he went down with a splat. After that, it felt like a hundred boots kicked him four ways from Sunday. The second hit to his head, he didn't know what it was that plowed him from behind, but it was just enough to knock him out.

Waking up in the infirmary, he didn't like that he was cuffed to the bed by his leg and wrist. However, when he tried to pull free, he realized that he was in the clinic for a reason. Every part of his body was hurting, and he could see blood on his gown.

Yelling for someone to come and let him loose, he had to close his eyes every time he even whispered as it sent a wave of pain in his head like he'd been slammed against a wall over and over. Then he remembered that he'd been hurt, that them men, whoever they were, had been naked as a jaybird wearing these big old boots and using them on him. What the hell caused them to do something like that, he wondered.

"Ain't no reason for anyone to be beating on me." He didn't yell anymore and was careful that his whispering didn't make his forehead crinkle up. He was fearful of touching his head because he didn't know what he'd find when he did that. This shit was for the birds. They must of used them boots on his face, is all he could figure.

"Damn it all to fuck and back. I don't

deserve this. I'm getting out today. They must be jealous. That's it. Jealous." Finally, someone came to see to him, and he was uncuffed. The man told him that shower time was over and that he had to do himself a spit bath. "That's the most disgusting thing. I ain't gonna spit on me to get clean. Where is your head at?"

"Not spit on you, moron but use a little water like a spit full and whip yourself up. Christ, why would anyone think you were to...just clean up. I'd not shave if I was you. You got you some stitches in your face, and it might hurt you more should you cut them open." The man walked away laughing, and Chad had a feeling that the whole world had gone stupid.

It took him nearly an hour and a whole lot of sweating to get himself dressed in a clean shirt and pants. The stains under his arms reached from his pits to his hem, and he didn't smell good again. Taking a bit of water, more than a spit full this time, he tried rinsing out his pit area so he'd at least be half clean. But when he was getting his boots on, he knew he'd not done himself a bit of good by wetting up the sweat smell again. He stank worse than a whore in a whore house as his momma used to say.

The ride over to the courthouse wasn't all that long. The cops, they said they were doing him a favor by letting him air out a bit by leaving the winders down. He thought all they'd done was muss up his hair a bit. The swirling smell about made him sick when it flew past his nose, but he was gonna be dried out when he got there, so it couldn't be that bad.

The first thing that he noticed was how crowded the room was. There wasn't an empty chair in the place. Then he spied the long table. There were three seats there, and he started to make a beeline toward them. Before he was even halfway there, some fat broad sat herself down in one of them and then had the nerve to smile at him. Like she knew all along that was his seat.

"You're to take a seat at the other table." The cop behind him gave him a little shove, but since he was chained up like some kind of wild animal, he nearly fell on his face by stumbling around on the chains. Turning to yell at the man, he saw something there that gave him pause. It was like his face had changed, just for a few seconds, into a lizard. Then he...he squirted his tongue out at him. "Yeah, you'd better behave. I'm in no mood to fuck with you today. No one in here cares a fig if you're tried or not. In fact, I'm betting about anyone who's heard about what you did to Saul's daughter. They'd just as soon string you up on their own."

He was careful how he stepped then. While Chad didn't know who this Saul person was—his name did ring a little bell in his head, he didn't know anybody's kids. Once he was seated, his hands chained to the table. He watched as the front of the room filled out, too. The judge was a damned woman too.

"Christ, oh mighty." She turned and looked at him, cocking her brow at him like she wasn't happy with his comment. "You're a woman. Ain't you got nothing better to do than to—I know that it's supposed to be old-fashioned or whatever to think women don't have a place out in the world, but I believe that they shouldn't be in places of authority. Isn't there...I don't know. Is your daddy around someplace that can take care of this courtroom stuff? Girls are just too emotional. You'll have me trussed up like a pig on slaughter day before we get to the reason why we're here.

The thing is, I just want you to make Chalina and Daughter to hand me over the money that should have rightly been mine. My momma died last and all dad's—I know, he's not my daddy, but his worldly goods should have gone to her then on to me. This ain't right that she didn't get anything."

"Mr. Chad Birkhimer, I'm assuming." He said that was him. "I was told that you were just wanting money that you have felt was stolen from you by way of your biological daughter and her mother. Well, I do have some terrible news for you. Even if your stepfather would have left your mother anything in the way of money, it wouldn't have made it to you. You wouldn't have received a penny of it due to her murdering those two people that day. Everything, and I mean even if the house had it been given to her, would have been sold off, and the proceeds plus the other money would have gone directly to the families that lost a loved one that day. Also, it's been brought to my attention as well that they're finding bodies—missing children and adults on the land that was Mr. Holt's, too, that can be connected to your mother killing them."

"How does that become my trouble? I didn't kill nobody off. She did all that on her own." The judge said that because neither she nor he was mentioned in the will, they weren't entitled to anything of Mr. Holts. "Well, that just can't be right. Also, that daughter of mine, she promised me her money, and she was going to be bailing me out. I was going to be living in the house with her and Chalina. I don't want to follow her rules, mind you, but we'll settle that up when you let me out of here. You're going to let me out of here, right? I got stuff to do with that money. And nothing is being done while I'm couped up like an animal here."

"You are an animal." Chad turned to look to see who had spoken about him. When he stood up, he remembered him being there when Daughter had been hurt. He'd threatened him, too, come to think of it. "Your honor, Mr. Birkhimer nearly killed my daughter the other day. As it stands now, she has been blinded by his actions. Lynn will need extensive surgeries to repair the damage that he did—"

"That's not your daughter, dumb shit. She's mine. And I didn't mean to hurt her that bad. I just asked her, polite like to shut up while I ate, and she didn't. I had to quiet her up, or I was going to have me a case of heartburn. If you've ever had that shit, you'd know that I was justified in quieting her down. Damn, but…" He turned back to the judge. "That's my daughter. She's the one I was telling you about. I'm going to get her money and live in the house with her. I'll need to get me a house of my own soon. Her jabbering all the time will get on a saint's last nerve, but like I said, we'll figure that out later. When you let me out of here."

"Let's just assume that you justified, as you said, for nearly killing Ms. Kennedy. Perhaps you can tell me why you killed Mr. Peabody." He asked her who that was. "The attorney that read the last will and testament of Mr. Holt. You bludgeoned him to death while he was headed to his car."

"Oh. He messed up reading the will, and I was—I didn't know that I was going to kill him. That wasn't my fault. He should have just done what I told him to do." She asked him if that was what he considered all right because the will didn't say what he wanted it to. "Of course. He would only have had to make sure that I got all the money, and that would have saved his life. He said that he'd not be able to practice law again if he told that little fib. That's all it was, too, a little fib. I did point out to him that he was an old fucker and didn't have much left in lawyering stuff to do. If you'd asked me, I think he needed a bit more practicing law on account of him not doing what is right. You know, now that I think on it, he wasn't dead when I was arrested. Somebody else must have killed him off when I wasn't looking. It happens, you know. People have a beef about their attorneys and kill them off when the opportunity comes up. And me giving him a few taps on the head, that didn't kill him. Someone else must have done that."

"The few taps to his head is what killed him, Mr. Birkhimer. Had you not hit him, he'd still be alive today." He just rolled his eyes at her. "Do you have anything else to say about what brought you here today? As far as I can tell, you've admitted to each of the crimes that were holding you in jail, and I'm ready to set a trial date for you."

"When do I get my money?" She asked him what money. "Ain't you been paying attention. The money that should have come to me when my mom died. You guys murdered her, but I'm not going to press any charges against you for that. It's made me a rich man, and I'm willing to forgive you for that."

"Your mother killed two people and was

killed before she could kill anyone else. That is what justifiable homicide is. She was about to kill a few more people if the list I have is any indication." He waved her off, telling her that she didn't, so it didn't count. "Mr. Birkhimer, I can tell you're related to your mother. You have the same traits that she has when it comes to having things your own way." She banged the gavel down and glared at him. Something else he didn't get was why everyone was so pissed off at him all the time. "You'll be remained over to the state penitentiary until your trial date arrives. I will set it in the morning. There is no reason for you to be here. Someone there will let you know when it is. Do you have an attorney, Mr. Birkhimer?"

"No. They sent me one, but I don't have any use for him on account of me not doing anything wrong. I just want you to make Chalina and Daughter to hand over the money that they stole from me, and I'm willing to forget all about this other stuff. Like someone killing off my momma." She said that no one was going to give him anything of the sort. "I hope you know that I'm not happy with the way you're treating me. That money should be mine."

"It's not. Move on. You'll be taken to prison as soon as you leave here until the trial. Court dismissed." She hit that little hammer on the table so hard that a piece of wood went flying off her table and to the floor. Scared him a bit. He thought for sure that she was trying to kill him. As soon as she was gone, he sat there for several minutes thinking about how things didn't go his way. There was no way that he was going to be spending another night in jail. He'd not done a damned thing.

Once he was chained up and put in a van this time, he thought for sure that she'd changed her mind and he was going home. There was a box of his things on the seat in front of him, and he asked if he could put the clothing on while they were driving. No one said anything, but he couldn't move as they'd already locked him down to the seat. He gave them the address of his house and watched as they drove right by it when he asked them to stop. Christ, people didn't listen to shit anymore.

~*~

"Can you tell me what I look like?" Saul asked Lynn if she had asked her mom. "I did. All she told me was that I was beautiful. She then told me that

I'd see it soon enough and that I would be all right then. Mom thinks that I'm going to be able to see out of the one eye. I believe that you'd tell me the truth. I hope so, anyway. I think being prepared if I do get to see it will be better. Do you think that I will?"

"No." Lynn nodded and didn't say anything. "You did tell me to be honest. There was a great deal of damage done to your face, honey, and even if you were to be able to shift right away, I don't think that there is enough there for your magic to repair the hurt that was done to your eye. I will tell you this. You're taking this a great deal better than I think that I'd be. You ask me, and I'll tell you. All right?"

"Yes, all right." She didn't say anything for a while, and he waited. When she took his hand into hers, he held her tightly until she was ready. "He hit my face on the bars. I know that, but after that, I don't know anything. The doctor said that they'd had to remove the eye on the one side because it had been crushed. Is that right?"

"Yes. You have a small face, naturally, because you're a child. Had you been an adult when he did that, you would have lost both eyes.

Because the bars were apart more than your eyes were, he only managed to hit the one and your cheek on the other side." Saul took a deep breath before speaking again. "I'm not sure if you were told this or not, but you have over four thousand stitches in your face and head. A great many of them are at the back of your head where they removed the tumor. It wasn't cancerous. Did they tell you that?"

"Yes. I know this sounds terrible, but I was hoping it would be so that I'd die. I don't...it's going to be hard to be a blind person after seeing all my life, I think." Saul told her that he had a friend who was born blind, and when he told him about how she'd been hurt, he said that he was envious of you knowing things. "Knowing things? I don't understand."

"Kyle, he's been blind since birth, as I said. He said that when someone told you that the sky was blue or that the grass was green, you'd be able to see that in your head. He can't. He's never seen colors or grass. To him, to most blind people, I imagine, it's difficult to imagine what green would be like." She said that she thought that it was sad that she'd never see the colors again. "Yes, that's very true. But you can imagine them when someone tells you that you look pretty in yellow. Which you do." She thanked him.

"Okay, so my face. Is it really scarred up?" He ever so gently touched her face where the stitches were. Telling her how far the line of them went to the bottom of her chin. Then he went to the other side and did the same thing. "The place in the back of my head. Will the scar show if I have my hair in a ponytail?"

"Right now, your head has been shaved all over. It's growing back, but only a bit of it is noticeable. I will tell you it makes you look worse than I think that it is. The wounds are showing more. But once your hair is back, I don't think you'll look nearly as beaten up. However, this I do know, that once you shift, not for a while yet, your hair will come in fully. We're still unsure of the scars and if they'll disappear once you shift."

He told her about the wounds on her chin that were stitched but looked healed. Explaining to her about her ears and how they'd had to stitch it back to her head once the tumor was taken out.

"Here, I brought you something." Pulling the golf ball out of his pocket, he put it in her hand.

"This is the size of the tumor that was removed. This ball is hard but the tumor that they removed was softer, I was told. It was smashed up against your skull and had even grown up and under it at the neckline. They—"

"Stop." He kissed her on the cheek where she wasn't hurt. "That was more than my mom told me, and while it's good to know, it's making my belly churn a little. Can I keep this ball? Just to remind myself how lucky I was?"

"Of course, you can keep it. I bought it for you anyway." He looked around the room. "A great many people have sent you flowers and cards. They're all over your room. Your mom mentioned that you love orchids, and at last count, you have ten plants of them. In an array of colors, too. There are cut flowers too. But some of them have been taken to other rooms so that they can enjoy them. You've gotten too many, and they were filling the room."

"I'm so glad that someone did that. I don't like cut flowers for that very reason. They die off." He got up and pulled a couple of cards off, and read them to her. "Is there fruit there? I keep smelling bananas and oranges. What I wouldn't give to be able to eat a banana right now."

"You can. However, it has to be in small smashed bites. Here, let me fix you one." After peeling the fruit, he used the spoon that was on her tray and smashed it up. After trying to judge how big of a bite to give her, he held it to her mouth while she nibbled on it. Her moan made him laugh. "If I cut you up a couple of grapes, would you like that too? But you can't chew them. Just suck the juice out of them and spit out the skin."

Lynn was so excited to have food, real food, she called it. She managed to eat half a banana as well as a half dozen grapes and sucked the juice out of half of an orange. She was so happy that his heart felt like it was beating just for her. After she said she had enough but to hide the spoon for next time, he did just that.

"I'll personally call the President and let him know how well his basket went over." She asked him if he really knew the president. "I do. He's been to the house a few times too. He's a very nice man. You'll get to meet him sometime."

He read the rest of the cards that came with the flowers and put them away in the drawer after writing a brief description on the back as to what the flowers looked like. There was one more basket of fruit, but it was dried things with nuts, and he didn't want to hurt her by feeding her some of that. When he sat down with her again, Saul asked her what else she wanted to know.

"Will you forgive me?" He was confused at first, then she explained. "I was a terrible person to you and to everyone else when I was ill. I want you to know that I'm so sorry for that. I never—"

"You have nothing to be sorry about, honey. Nothing at all. After you had your surgery, your mom and I looked up about what to expect after that kind of thing happened. More often than not, it doesn't get noticed until a person goes completely insane from it, and by then, it's too late. I'm just thrilled beyond words that it was found in time, and you're not having many side effects with it being removed." She asked him what kind of side effects. "The person goes completely off the rails and ends up killing a lot of people. When asked about it, they say that they spend every waking hour thinking about how to kill off people. They don't even have to piss them off. They just want to kill. In others, the tumor gets so large that it cuts off the blood to the brain. The vessel then fills with blood if it can't find a different direction to go, and they die of a brain bleed. That's mostly what happens to children. It just bursts, and that's it."

"So even though he hurt me badly, I'm lucky that he did what he did." Saul said that was true but not to say that to anyone else. "No. I think it would hurt Mom if I were to say that to her. She cries a lot when she's here. She thinks that just because I can't see her, I can't hear her either. It hurts me when she cries. It wasn't her fault."

"But she's your mom, and no matter what you say to her, she's going to feel like she's failed you. My dad, he told me the same thing. That it didn't matter how it happened or who did it, he'd feel guilty for the rest of his life if something like that had happened to one of us." She told him that his dad came in daily and read her the newspaper. "He told me. I don't know why he'd think that you'd be interested in the world news, but he's always in a good mood when he gets home."

"Everyone has been in at some point over the last few days. Sherm visits me the most. I can't believe how smart he is. He told me the other day that being here with me had made him want to become a brain surgeon. I guess when the doctor had finished up with my head, Sherm asked him some good questions. He even allowed him to go to the teaching surgery room so that he could observe. With his parents' permission, I guess." She took a deep breath, and he prepared himself for whatever she was going to say to him. "Can I call you Dad? I don't deserve it, not so soon after being so mean to you. But you've been a better dad to me than Chad—what I'm going to call him from now on—has ever been to me. Even when I was little. You don't have to say yes. Grandda, your dad said that it was all right with him that I called him that. I've never had—Can I call you Dad, please?"

"Yes. I'd be honored for you to call me that. And I'm betting that my dad has told everyone in town that he has the prettiest granddaughter now. I'm going to take out a full page in the paper to let the world know that you're my daughter." They both laughed. "Please, call me Dad. I have always felt, even when you screamed at me not to call you my daughter, that you were my child." She said she was sorry again. "Don't be. Don't ever be sorry for what happened. You're better now, and that is all that matters."

Chalina showed up, bringing dinner for him and her. Lynn enjoyed some more fruit and her mom had brought her a smoothie that she was okayed to have. By the time she was finished with her dinner, Lynn was dozing off. Which he knew was good for her as rest would heal her quicker than anything. He and Chalina talked about nothing much, and he was happy that they both decided to stay the night with Lynn so if she woke up afraid, they'd be there for her.

"The doctor called today. He said that if things kept progressing the way that they are, we should be able to bring her home on Thursday. I'm so excited. And I'm glad that you had one of the rooms downstairs set up for her temporarily. It'll be nice having her home." Saul agreed with her. "I don't know that I'll be able to sleep any better, but I was wondering if you'd sleep with me tonight and forever. I want to have you next to me when I have nightmares, too."

"I'll gladly do that for you." After Chalina fell asleep, he pulled out his laptop and began working on some of the projects that he'd been putting off. While he was at it, he also emailed Caitlynne to see if she could get them a staff other than just a cook. Things were moving along, and he was thrilled beyond words that he was able to do this little bit of work for his new family.

Chapter 5

This kiss wasn't like the others Saul had given her. Those were tame in comparison, while this one felt more possessive and hungrier. She felt her own hunger soar, meeting his for every touch of his mouth.

They'd only been home one night, tonight. Coming here to make sure that things were set up for Lynn when she was discharged from the hospital had been her idea. But Saul had pulled her to him, needing a hug, he told her when she wrapped her arms around his shoulders. Needing him, the permanence of his lovemaking in her heart, she asked him to kiss her again.

He demanded the entrance to her mouth this time, his tongue sliding along her lips and pushing inside when she opened to him. He moaned deep, and she felt it rumble along her body through his chest to her own. Pressing her back against the mattress and covering her body with his heavy weight, he took several deep breaths because she knew that he might hurt them. She knew that she might well have, too, as needy as she was.

His hand moved down her ribs and then along her ass, pulling her hard and up into him. She could feel the hardness of his cock through the clothing that they both still had on. Sliding her leg up his to hook around him, but she wasn't able to because of the stupid clothing she had on.

"Christ, I want you. You're hot, and I can smell you, your arousal. I need to taste you. Now I need to taste." He began to move down her body, licking and nipping at her as he went tearing off her clothing piece by piece as he did. By the time he had settled himself between her legs, she was wild with a need of her own.

She leaned up on her elbows as he sat on his feet. His cock was hard and sticking straight out from his groin. It was an impressive cock too. One that she thought would hurt her if he were to take her right now. As she watched him, he wrapped his hand around the shaft and pumped his hand up and down. A drop of cum seeped from the tip. She licked her lips, a need to take him into her mouth making her hungry and aggressive. Something that she'd never been with anyone else. She started forward, reaching for him, and he stopped her.

"No. Not yet. I would like nothing better than to have you wrap your mouth around me, but I want to taste you, all of you. Next time, I promise you'll be able to do what you want, but next time. Oh sweetheart, you're wet, so wet I can see the dampness on your curls." He let go of his cock and touched her pussy. As much as she wanted to roll her eyes in the back of her head and pass out, she knew instinctively that he wasn't finished with her.

His finger moved slowly along her nether lips, up and down like he had his cock. Her body responded, and she felt her pussy weep more. He hadn't touched her yet, not touched her where she needed. When his finger slowly entered her heat, she opened her legs wider and raised her hips up to meet him.

"Please, Saul. I want you. I...there's a need, something...I don't... you have to fill it for me, please, fill me." Her hips moved up and down with his finger, and when he inserted another into her heat, she nearly came up off the bed. Whimpering now, she moved faster with his fingers deep inside of her. It was both too much and not nearly enough.

"I need to stretch you love. You're too tight to take me inside of you yet. That's what you want, me to fill you with my cock, isn't it?" He was moving faster now; her body was on fire.

"Yes, oh yes, please." She felt rather than saw him move, her body straining to get to something. When she felt his breath on her thigh, she started to clamp her legs closed, but he held them open with his hands. She was panting now, her need making her ach for release.

With his fingers, he opened her lips and ran his tongue inside her, lapping at her, tasting her. When his mouth closed over her clit and suckled into his mouth, she screamed out her climax, but he didn't stop. While his fingers fucked her, his mouth teased and nipped at her until she came again and again.

"Please, Saul, please. I want you; I want to suck your cock. Now I want you to come in my mouth." As she reached for him, pulling away from his very talented tongue, she pushed him back against the footboard. She leaned forward and stroked the length of him with just the tips of her fingers. His hiss made her bolder.

"Take me, love. Take me in your mouth. I want to fuck your hot mouth and shoot cum deep into your throat."

She swiped her tongue across the tip of the large, deep purple head, taking the cream into her mouth. He hissed again. Bolder than she had ever been in her life, she wrapped her lips around him and licked again. She loved the way he responded. He pumped into her. She didn't know what she was doing, but taking her cues from him and his body, she licked and nipped every inch of him, up one side of him, then down the other. When she felt his hand touch the back of her head, she felt him guide her, show her what he needed. Soon he was pumping into her hard, his cock bumping the back of her throat again and again. His hips were moving faster and faster, and she knew he was close to coming.

"I'm going to come to Chalina. Fuck, I'm coming!" Seconds later, she felt the first hot explosion hitting the back of her throat. He pumped harder into her, pulsing into her over and over. She swallowed him, his cum; loving the salty taste that she knew was unique to him. He lifted her up and turned her over onto her hands and knees. She was ready, she thought, so ready for his cock to be deep inside of her. Moaning, she moved back against him.

"Please, Saul, I need you inside me. I need to feel you inside me."

"Beg for it." He growled in her ear, his fingers teasing her lips apart and then one finger slid inside her ass. He rubbed his length along her wetness, teasing her by not pushing inside. "I need you to beg me, Chalina. Tell me that you're mine, and I'll give you what you want." His voice was thick with desire, sending shivers down her spine.

"Oh, Saul...I'm yours, only yours. Please... complete me." She moaned as she arched her back, inviting him in.

With one swift thrust, he penetrated her to the hilt, filling her completely and stretching her walls around his girth. The slight pain melted away as pleasure consumed her senses. Her nails dug into the bedding as she cried out his name in ecstasy and agony. He held still for a moment, allowing her to adjust before he started to move again, slow at first, but picking up speed with each thrust. His hips slapping against her ass echoed in the room, sending waves of anticipation through her body.

His hands gripped her hips tightly as he angled his penis to hit that sweet spot deep within her. "Fuck...you feel so...incredible...so...tight... around me." He groaned, his breathing ragged in her ear.

"I...I can't...it's too much..." she panted, on the verge of another orgasm.

"That's it...let go...come for me...I want to feel your...tight pussy milking my cock." His words sent her over the edge, her orgasm crashing over her like a tidal wave. Her pussy contracted around him, milking his length as he cried out and spilled his seed inside her depths.

Saul collapsed on top of her, their heavy breathing mingling in the air. His weight didn't bother her; she wanted to feel him against her forever. His cock still hard within her, she knew this night was far from over. Then she felt him stiffen behind her, felt his anger roll off him and into her.

"It's the fucking prison calling me again. Christ, I wish he would just serve his time without making us suffer too." He turned her in his arms and kissed her. "I want you to know that I'm not nearly finished with you yet. I don't know that I ever will be. But if he doesn't back off, he's going to disappear."

She giggled. When Saul smiled at her, she felt as if she could take on the world. There was some doubt that she would come out on top, but she knew that she could take on someone and feel good and strong about doing it. Chalina was in love, and she couldn't have found a more perfect person to be in love with either.

~*~

"I demand that you get me that Tate person. Saw or something like that." The officer with him told him that he could call him on Thursday. "It's Friday. I don't want to wait a whole week to call him. He has some things he said he'd do for me. I want him to…he's going to have to get me out of here. I don't care for being here."

"Well, la-dee-da. No one wants to be in prison. Deal with it. And it's not Friday, it's Thursday. You were told four times yesterday by me that it was Wednesday. There is no telling how many more people said it to you between me and the others." He asked him when he could make his call. "Today. Sometime after lunch. We don't want you waking up everyone too early with your calls. You can't be that sick of us. You've only been here for a week."

"This is the worst place I've ever been. And I've been in prison before. I ain't got me a decent meal once. My mattress is floppy — like a hundred other people have slept on it. Have they?" The officer told him that everybody got new mattresses. "Well, I didn't. I didn't get anything new when I got here, and that's just gross. I think I'm even wearing someone else's underwear. They got the name Hanes or something like that written in them."

"You do, too, have a new mattress, and the name in your underwear is Hanes because that's who the manufacturer is, not who wore it last." Chad was pretty sure he was wrong about that but didn't comment. The only company that made underwear was Fruit on the Moon. And these weren't that. "When it's your turn to make a call, I'll come and get you. Remember, you have to have the phone number because we're not a switchboard."

When the man walked away, he stuck his tongue out at him. There wasn't any point in yelling, that would get him in trouble, and he had enough of that going around as it was. Yesterday, he'd been hosed down with a fire hose on account of him not wanting to clean up his cell. Well, the sucker was clean now, by golly. His mattress was damp and the extra clothing that he'd had tossed in the corner had taken all day and into the night before they were just damp. This place had a hard way in making you follow the rules. That's why he needed to talk to Saw.

On his first day here somebody had pointed out that his daughter, he never did know her name, was going to be adopted by the Tates. And more than likely his ex-whatever, he wasn't sure what to call Chalina was gonna be marrying one of them too.

Somebody would have to be a damned fool to not know who they were. The Tates had all the money and wasn't above sharing it with the masses if you showed them how much you needed it. He surely did need it. Somebody, he didn't know who that might be, was going to have to give him enough money to get out of prison. It wasn't a place he wanted to be.

Laughing a little to himself, he knew that if anyone deserved to be in prison, it would have been him. He'd killed off enough people that if he only had to spend one year in prison for killing someone, he'd be there for fifty or more years. Chad's motto was if you got in his way, he'd murder you. That had gotten him by for all his life, and he didn't feel the need to change things up now.

He'd also been in on a couple of bank robberies, liquor store heists, and a lot of household invasions. While he'd do the household ones, he didn't really care for them. They were easy and quick, but they yielded very little in the way of cash or even goods. He and his buddy had once spent an entire week in watching this house, only to find out that it was a front for a mobster's place. It was filled with room after room of televisions still in the box, refrigerators as well as dishwashers and the like. Nothing that they could move out easily without being caught. They nearly had got caught, too.

Just as the two of them were thinking that they were in the wrong house, the front door opened up. Then the garage door started its noisy slide up the tracks, exposing his buddy trying to get new boxes of tools stuffed in the plastic trash bags they'd found. The bags weren't worth spit as they kept tearing in half. However, the door going up nearly made his nuts crawl right up his ass and replacing his throat bumps in the back of his mouth.

He'd hit the floor like he'd been pegged to it, but Tommy, dumber than a two-headed snake, just stood there with his bag ripped to shreds, his mouth hanging open and staring right at the man himself. Michael Sterner, the biggest mob boss in the whole entire state of Ohio.

There were two small popping sounds, and Tommy hit the floor, too. But most of the back of his head was gone from the two holes in his cheeks just under his eyes. The bugger was staring right at him as if he was telling Sterner where he was.

Shimming under the big car that was in the garage, he kept an eye on the feet, making their way up to Tommy and sliding his ass out of the garage and to the side of the house. For another twenty minutes or so, he stood there, sweating like it was full-on summer when it was about ten degrees out, hoping that no one would notice that he'd peed himself and was smearing it out to his place he had been hiding under that big old caddy.

"You got the number?" He nearly screamed when the officer spoke to him. Bringing him out of his thoughts like he had made Chad reach for his gun. Not that he'd carried one for the last few years. They were getting harder to come by, too, since every mother fucker in the world had to have one.

People didn't realize that you couldn't just keep using the same one over and over but had to replace it, or that would surely get you caught. They could run some kind of forest test on it— something about shooting the bullet into water or such to tell it was the same gun. Plus, bullets were expensive. He was asked again if he had the number?

"Yeah. Yeah, I got it." He made his way to the phone that was in a little office. When he'd been in prison the first time at seventeen, they had the kind that hung on the wall to use. Now, they had one that sat on the desk with buttons to push.

It was still old-fashioned, but it did the job. Dialing the number that he had on a bitty piece of paper, he had to ask the officer what one of the numbers was. "Okay. Yeah, zero. I didn't know you could use that number in phone numbers. I thought it was just for emergencies." Apparently not. Almost as soon as he got the numbers dialed in, someone answered. He asked to speak to Saw.

"Mr. Tate is at the office this morning. May I take a message for him? Or would you like to speak to Mrs. Tate?" He didn't know if whoever Mrs. Tate would help him, but he was only going to get this one call this week. After telling the man that was fine, he waited.

"Hello, this is Chalina Tate. Can I help you?" Surely he didn't hear that right, did he? He'd done went and married Chalina? That wasn't— "Hello? Is someone there?"

"It's Chad Holt. Or I guess Berkheimer. Where is your husband? I need to speak to him about getting me out of here. You're too mean to work with. Get him for me." When he realized that Chalina was laughing, he wanted to hang up on her. But remembered just barely that this was his call. "Damn it, Chalina, why do you have to piss me off all the time? Where is Saw? Who names their kid that anyway? His parents must have been wood cutters, is all I can think of."

"He's working. And it's not SAW but SAUL." He didn't notice a damned thing different even after she spelled it for him but told her again to get her husband on the phone. "I already told you, Chad, he's at work. And as for getting you out of prison, that's not going to happen. We all like it just where you are. In fact, if we could add more time to your sentencing, we'd do that. How did you get this number anyway? I certainly didn't give it to you."

"That kid did. Well, I don't think she meant for me to have it, but it was on some of the papers she brought here to see me. She had a whole bunch of rules written out that I was supposed to follow, but that ain't going to happen. I make the rules, not some snot-nosed kid." Chalina said she was hanging up. "You are not. You get me in touch with your husband, or so help me, Chalina, I'm going to make you regret messing with me."

"I regret every second of my life that I had with you anyway. Except for you giving me my child. She's the only good thing that came from you." He thanked her. "You bastard, I'm not thanking you for her. What do you want my husband for?"

"He needs to get his ass down here and get me out of this mess I'm in. I no more deserve being in prison than he does." He paused a moment. "Should he be in prison? I mean, he does have a lot of money, I'm told. I'd like to have me a pitcher of that."

"No, he shouldn't be in prison. You're such a dumbass. It's picture, not pitcher. One you get a drink from the other is having something thrown at your empty head. And since I've told you this before, I do believe you were dropped on your head a great deal when you were younger. We love where you are. You're not hurting us, any of us, and I don't have to keep looking over my shoulder to see where you are all the time." She sounded like she was crying. "Don't you dare call here again, do you hear me? No one is going to help you out of prison, and we're certainly never going to help you with any kind of funds for any reason. You made your bed. Now you lie in it."

Before he could complain to her about the bed he had and the floppy mattress, she hung up on him. Hung up like he wasn't talking to her. He sat there for five minutes, wondering what he was to do now that he'd made his call when he decided to ring her back. Just as he was pulling out the number to call her back, the phone rang. It scared ten years off his life when he picked it up to answer.

"Who is this?" He didn't know the man's voice, but he could tell that he was angry. After telling him his name, the man started cursing at him. "What the hell do you think you're doing calling my wife and upsetting her? She was just beginning to sleep well and through the night, and you have to go and call her. What the hell is wrong with you?"

"I want you to come here and get me out of this situation that you put me in." He asked him how he thought it was his fault that he was in prison. "You didn't give me any money to be bailed out. You Tates, you have enough. It wouldn't have bothered you one bit to have slipped some money to the honor guy and told him to let me go. I might not have bothered you none had you done that. But you can bet I will now. You get your ass down here and—hello? Hello? Damn it, you had better not hung up on me. That's rude. Do you hear me? That's just plain rude."

"Who are you talking to?" Chad told the officer that he'd been talking to Saw Tate when the line was disconnected. "You mean he hung up on you. That makes more sense than you telling me that it was disconnected. Come on, your call is finished."

"No, it's not. I tell you, we were disconnected." The officer said it was because Saul hung up. "No, he didn't. You don't know Jack shit. I was the one talking to him. Let me call him back, and you can ask him. I'm not going anywhere because of the two calls I made. Neither of them said they'd help me."

"You made two calls?" He nodded before he realized that he told on himself. "Well, ain't that nice for you. I guess you won't be making any calls next week, then. You were told you could only have—"

"That is the stupidest rule I've ever heard. Why can't I make as many calls as I want? Huh? It's not like they're lined up here to make calls. Most of the people in here don't have a pot to piss in, much less someone to come and bail them out.

I have family out there. Did you know that I'm related to the Tates? They're getting together right now to get me out of here."

The mike on the officer's shoulder went off, and Chad had a difficult time understanding what was being said. Something about Tate and a saw. Might have been the man's name. But when he said *out*, like he was going to be taking him out, Chad let himself get excited. Was he already getting out? He looked at the officer when he jerked him up from the chair.

"You're not to call the Tates again. They said that if you did, then they were going to come down here and have a meeting with you. I don't think it's going to be a good meeting either. Mr. Tate said that you threatened him and that he didn't take kindly to that." He asked when he'd threatened him. "You told him that when you got out, you were going to bother him every day."

"Yeah, I did say that, but I was only kidding him." He was taken back to his cell, trying to convince the officer that he'd only been joking around and that the man had a board up his ass and didn't know how to take a joke all that well. "Are you really not going to let me make a call next week? I gotta let them know that I'm not happy with the way that they're treating me."

"You are banned from making any calls in the foreseeable future. Now, sit down and shut up. You've caused enough trouble for one day. I don't want to hear another word from you for the rest of the night." He banged his baton on the bars that sent a ringing in his ears that hurt. "Stay quiet, and you might just live through the night."

He didn't like that, being threatened like he was some kind of monster, but he didn't say anything. After the officer walked away, telling everyone that he passed that lights would be out at ten tonight, he flipped him off. Of course, he was careful of not being seen, but still, he felt better just being able to do that one thing that made him feel like he had won something.

Chad was going to have to figure out a way to get back at that man Saw. He was rude as hell, and he didn't care for him. He thought of all kinds of plans to get the man to see things his way, and the only one that he could come up with that would work was to get Daughter to do it for him. She still owed him that money she promised him, and it was high time that he collected on it.

~*~

Saul had a lot going on right now, and he couldn't concentrate on any of it because he'd had to deal with a man who should have been put out of their misery months ago. Not even with Chad being in prison did he stop. He looked at the doorway when he heard the tapping of Lynn's cane.

"There's a chair right in front of you if you'd like to have a seat." She told him that she wanted to talk to him about something. "Sure. You know that you're welcome to come to me at any time."

She'd been going to classes to learn how to get around for the last two weeks since she'd gotten settled in at home. After the first week, she wanted her room back upstairs. Lynn was trying her best to normalize her life. Sherm, his nephew, was helping her, too. The kid was brilliant, and the two of them, with their heads together, made him feel good. When she was seated in his office chair — it was difficult for him not to pick her up and carry her everywhere — she turned to talk to him.

"I'm just going to tell you. I want to be able to help others like me." He leaned back in his chair and waited for her to explain. Something that he'd come to realize about Lynn and her mom was that they didn't like to be rushed when they had something to say. "Sherm, he's been coming to visit me almost every day, as you know, and we talked about me being able to remember colors and textures. Do you remember you telling me about your friend? I told Sherm about him. So I want to help. Before, I was blind, I mean. He seems to think, and I think he might be right, that I can help others who were blind from birth. Sherm said that I could help people realize the colors of simple items. He said that they can feel the grass, but they don't know what green is." She smiled at him. "Am I screwing this up? I'm kind of nervous."

"No, not at all. I love all this. It's an excellent idea. I've noticed that you've been touching a lot of things that are around the house. Are you trying to get a feel for them or thinking about how to explain to someone what it might be? Either way, that's a wonderful thing to want to do." She told him that she was actually feeling things like it was the first time she'd seen it. "Okay. But I don't understand."

"When I could see, I knew what a book would feel like. How the pages felt when I turned them. But I never thought of how the pages made a sound when you turned them. How much heavier the covers were even if it was a paperback. The feel of silverware. Sure, I know what a fork is, but now I think about its weight and textures that mark it as a set. If it's balanced. That's important to me now. The balance of things." She frowned. "I don't think I'm saying this right."

"Oh, but you are, honey. I understand. You're saying that you've gotten a new outlook on things that you took for granted before. Like you said, the weight of things. The way it might feel in your hands. I love that idea." She blushed, and he smiled, knowing better than to laugh. She was still tender about her emotions. "I'm assuming that between the two of you, you have a plan."

"Yes. Sherm helped me put together a plan that I'm going to send to the local school for the blind. I wanted to get your opinion on it since you know how to write up a business plan. I don't need the money if they want to pay me, but if they insist, I'm going to use it to buy some things that I can use to help them out." He told her that wherever she went, they'd supply her with the items she needed. "Oh. I didn't know that. But that makes sense. Then I don't know. Maybe something for the school."

"Excellent idea. I'll help you with that too in your plan. Also, you should think about learning brail. I know that you've been working with it with your mom but you'll need to be professional at it when you're in a classroom setting. You know, I'm very proud of you and Sherm. You're both so young but taking on projects that a much older person might not have thought about." She told him that Sherm had gotten her some books that she could read that she knew by heart. "Good plan. I like that. You've really given this a good deal of thought, Lynn, I'm proud of you. I bet your mom is too."

"I hope she will be. She kind of hovers over me all the time, so I'm not sure how she'll take me going to school with the blind." She wiped at the tears that were falling, and he wanted to get up and hug her. "I sometimes find myself feeling sorry for myself. A lot. I don't like that feeling. I don't…being blind is so different than…I'm going to miss out on a lot of things that I never thought of before. Like seeing Mom's face when she's happy. Getting to drive a car. I know that it's silly, but—"

"It's not silly, Lynn. It's normal to feel sorry

for what you've lost. And even though you have your health, you still lost a great part of yourself by not being able to see and having that taken away from you so violently." She had shifted three days ago, and while all her scaring was gone, her eye was just too damaged to be repaired by her magic. "You need anything else, you just come to see me, and between the three of us, we'll get this on the road to happening."

When she said she was going to go up to her room, he watched her until she got to the top of the stairs. When she made her way down the hallway toward her room, he turned and nearly ran into his dad, who had come into the house at some point.

"I was wondering if you have a few minutes." He hugged his dad, telling him that he had all the time in the world for him. "Yeah, I'm getting that a lot from the others. You boys, you sure do make a man happy to be a dad all the time. Don't be getting me all sloppy. I need your help on some projects I got going in my head."

His dad, a great note-taker when he had an idea or just something that he wanted to jot down, pulled out his notebook and laid it on his leg. He fussed around with it for about ten minutes before he finally looked at him.

"Now. I don't want you just telling me that you'll do this for me if you think it's what I want to hear, all right." He told him that he'd never do that. "Yes, you would. All of you would. And I understand you wanting me to be happy. But I don't want to look stupid either. All right."

"Dad, if anyone ever thinks that one of your ideas is stupid, I want you to tell me who it is. Because I don't want to beat them for thinking that you're stupid, but I want to meet the man that has to be stupider than even that ex-husbands of Chalina if they don't think that you're as brilliant as we all know you to be."

"You're a good son, Saul." Dad blew his nose noisily and smiled then. "You always were. Now, about this here project. I want you to tell me if having one of those activity parks like bigger cities have would be welcomed around here."

"Activity parks for the young or anyone that comes by?" He was already on board with the idea because there was nothing like that around here. Not even a very good bike path that someone could take a long walk on. "I can see the benefits of both kinds, but you tell me what you had in mind, and we'll work from there."

After an hour of them making more notes and then finding a plot of land to put it all on, they were well on their way to looking up prices on swing sets for small children and adults. The part that he loved the most was Dad's idea of having a couple of vendors there on the weekends to sell ice cream cones as well as cold sandwiches with chips. It would require hiring a few people to work through the summer months in addition to a lifeguard if they went with a pool and whatever else they could come up with.

"I can see having some little buildings to talk about trees and some of the creatures that live around this area. How to take care of yourself when you're out and about." Saul wanted to get a start on it now, going to buy a bulldozer to do the work himself just to get a jump on it. Dad, his wonderful dad, told him that he could use it with supervision and permission from Chalina as well.

"Spoilsport." Laughter from his dad was always a highlight of his day. And right now, the two of them had been laughing quite a bit. He loved this project and the time he could spend with his dad and wondered if his brothers got the same feeling when they hung out with him.

Chapter 6

Chalina didn't want to be here today. She had started enjoying being at home all the time in the event someone needed her. But cleaning out their other place, just a two-bedroom apartment, had to be done, and she had decided to do it today. Lynn had come with her, which was good, too, but she'd put restrictions on her that she was to follow. Lynn wanted her to stop hovering over her all the time.

Hearing something hit the floor for the second time, she started counting. Lynn said that if, after the count of ten, she didn't say she was all right, then she could come to see what happened. She only got to four before Lynn said she was all right. Damn it, Chalina thought, she didn't like the independence of her daughter one bit.

"You're doing really well, Mom." That did

make her feel better, but she was getting ready to go to see to her anyway, but Lynn continued. "I dropped the box of paints that I had on my desk. They're all closed up, so I'm not worried about the stains, but could you come here and make sure that I got them all? I don't want to step on them and break them."

"Gladly." Finding her daughter on the floor with her back to her gave her a small pause. "You're getting so big now that I hardly recognize you."

"Dad said that my hair would grow back the first time I shifted, and I'm so glad that it did. He told me I look less wounded now because the wounds are all closed up and gone. The only scar that I still have is the one along my hairline, he told me." Lynn had been going to Saul when she needed advice. Like if her hair was straight down her back when she pulled it into a ponytail. Did her socks match? Not that it mattered, she didn't think if they matched, she would wear them anyway. "Mom, what are you thinking about? I'm all right, you know."

"I know you are. And to be honest, I wasn't really thinking of anything other than you doing right by going to Saul with your style questions. I was taking over when it wasn't perfect." She laughed, and Lynn joined her. "He pointed out that I tend to not answer you but to redo whatever it is that you ask me about. He said that annoyed you. I'm so glad that the three of us are going through this together. I can't think of a better male counterpart than Saul to be so calming about everything."

"One thing that I learned from grandda is that nothing will ever be perfect, so I might as well let the little stuff go. Not his exact words, but close enough. I used to do my homework, which had to be turned in several times so that there wasn't a single smudge or an eraser mark on it. Now, I'm happy with whatever I do because I did it to the best of my ability without stressing myself out too much. Even though my abilities have changed, I'm okay with being messy, too. Understand?" Nodding and then remembering to say yes, she sat down by Lynn when she saw one of the tubes of paint. Handing it to her, Lynn smiled. "Thank you for being my mom. Thank you so much for sticking with me when I was hurting and hurting everyone around me."

"It was my pleasure." Wiping at the tears, she asked Lynn what else she wanted to take home with her that was in her room. "I see that you have a pile on your bed that is mostly clothing. Do you want it or not?"

"Not. But I think I'm going to take it with me to donate to the clothing drive. I didn't know that they saved all those clothing parts to make quilts. I might not be able to see the beauty of them, but I do remember the prints on some of my shirts and dresses that might be used, and I can imagine its beauty." Again, she nodded but couldn't speak over the lump in her throat. Her daughter was growing up, and she was seeing things in ways to help others, too. "Sherm wants me to bring home my bow and arrow set. I was pretty good at it when I used it last. He seems to think that I will be, too, even though I'm blind. I don't know about that, but I think if anyone can help me make it work, it would be him."

"I agree." She helped Lynn sort out some of the other things that were in her room. Books were going with them so that other family members could read them. Her computer had already been packed up for her. Then there were the things that she didn't remember even having. Those were tossed into a box for donations, too. "If you don't remember them, it means you probably won't miss them if you don't take them with you."

"Yeah, that's right." The three of them were going to spend the night in the apartment and finish up tomorrow. Saul, who was on another business trip, was going to come to them tonight, and they were going to wait around for the trucks to come by in the morning to pick up all the donated furniture that they were getting rid of. Even food that was in the cabinets was being donated, and she felt really good about that.

It was nearly one when they decided to break for lunch. They'd never been broke, but they'd been close at times to not being able to afford food. Chalina made sure after the second time that it happened that it never happened again. All because of Chad getting into her account, they had an emergency box that would feed them for a few days deep in their closets. She knew that being married to Saul that wouldn't ever be a problem for them again.

The food was good, but she had gotten so used to having homemade foods that it tasted sort of bland. Lynn was doing much better with being able to eat different things now, but she still had some trouble with her upper teeth. Each time she would shift, something else would be repaired, and she was so happy about that.

"Mom, do you and Saul plan to have any more children?" Chalina told her that they'd talked about it, but they were still learning what kind of kids they'd have. "Yeah, I heard that Hanna say something about that. She's sort of scary, isn't she?"

"I find them all to be kind of scary if you want the truth." They both laughed, and it felt good. "I love them all, however. They're the nicest people in the world, don't you think?"

"Yes. Grandda asked me if I would help him out with the playgrounds that they're putting in. I don't know what I can do to help him. I've never been to a playground before but for school, but he said that I could help him with the safety aspects of being blind. He told me that he'd feel really terrible if someone got hurt because he didn't think of swings being too close to one of the other workout equipment because they didn't know to look out for them. I suggested that he put a bell on the swing to warn someone they were being used. He laughed for nearly an hour. I kid you not because it was so simple."

"It's brilliant. And like he said, so simple." They talked about her upcoming start to her new school. It was in Columbus, an hour away, so she was going to be living on campus. Most of the kids there did anyway, but Chalina didn't care for her being so far away. "Your uniforms came yesterday. They're very nice but very boring. They're blue and white."

"Who is going to care? It's not like anyone can see them." That made her laugh. Again, it was simple and truthful. "They said that once I get there, someone will come in and code my clothing. They said that I should do that at home. I don't know why I'd care what I look like around the house. I'm sure that you or Dad will tell me if I look like a hobo or something."

Her daughter had matured so much since her being hurt. She didn't laugh as much as she did before, but she seemed smarter and calmer. Chalina wondered if it was because that tumor had been there long enough that it was affecting her for a lot longer than anyone had realized. Chalina loved her daughter so much that she was thankful daily that she had her.

After cleaning up their lunch mess, they started on the rooms again. The apartment wasn't all that big, but she'd not realized how much crap they'd crammed into the place. Once she had the kitchen all cleared up and things put in boxes, she went to her room to get some of the clothing boxed up as well. When her cell phone rang, it startled her enough that she screamed. It had been so quiet all day that she'd forgotten about it.

"I'm calling you because I wanted to see if you were alone." She sat down on the side of the bed and asked him what was going on, that Lynn was still in her room. "Chad was killed about an hour ago. The details are sort of vague, but he apparently bit off more than he could chew, and one of the inmates beat him to death with a chair. He, the man who killed him, was killed by the guards when he wouldn't stop beating Chad even after he was long gone."

"What happens now? I mean, do you have any idea what will happen to all the crap that he did to other people? They won't get justice, will they?" He told her that he thought that everyone would be thrilled, but sadly that he had gotten what he deserved by being killed the way that he had. "I can see that. He is dead, and that has to be a relief to everyone that he hurt. Especially since he got a taste of his own sort of justice."

"That's what I'm thinking, too." He laughed a little. "Change of subject. I'm going to be a little later tonight than I thought. I'll be there in the morning first thing. Something with the house came up and I have to go and get it approved. Caitlynne is having a secure internet connection put into the house, and that will require my approval. I like the idea of us having a network that is safe for us all. But it's messing with my plans to take you to bed and fuck you until we're both nothing but a puddle of mush."

"I love the way your mind works." Lynn came into the room, and she told Saul that she had to go. "I'll see you in the morning." After she put her phone down, she looked at her daughter and waited for her to speak first.

"He's gone, huh?" Nodding, she waited for her daughter to ask her about his death. "I don't care. I mean, I really am glad that he's gone, but I feel guilty for thinking that. Not that he would have felt anything for what he did to me. But I do feel a little guilty."

"I understand that. I don't feel anything for him either. Less since he hurt you, but I'm glad that he's gone. Even from prison, he was a pain in our asses." Lynn smiled. "There's my little girl."

"I'm not exactly your little girl anymore, but I love that you call me that." She didn't leave, Chalina thinking that she had more to say yet. "Mom, I want to die."

Shocked, she couldn't speak yet, and Lynn started to leave her. Asking her to give her a moment to think, Lynn stood by the doorway as if she was going to bolt if Chalina said the wrong thing.

"Do you feel like that all the time? I mean, have you a plan to end your life?" Shaking her head, Lynn wiped at her tears as they fell. "I don't know what to say other than to beg you not to do anything without talking to me or Saul."

"I do. Talk to dad. No offense, Mom, but he doesn't freak out when I talk to him about being so sad all the time. You didn't this time, but I have tried to talk to you before." It hit her then that her daughter had been thinking about this for some time. Telling her that she was sorry only had Lynn crying more. "You don't have to be sorry. I just—I don't want you to tell me that I can't do that, can't have those thoughts. Just listen to me. Like Dad does. I've never told him that I want to die, but I do talk to him about how incredibly sad I am all the time. He doesn't say much, but he does listen to me and asks me all kinds of questions. I feel better when I leave talking to him, but it's getting worse all the time. I need help."

While she sobbed, Chalina got up and pulled her daughter into her arms. She'd been thinking that she was being so brave, but instead, she'd been begging her for help since the beginning. Holding her, she told her that she loved her and wouldn't know how to go on without her. But she did make sure that she knew that she'd do whatever she needed to get her some help.

"I want to go away. Not away, but I want to go to the hospital so that I can...I want someone to tell me what I'm supposed to do with these feelings. Acting on them, sometimes, it is all I can do to make myself get out of bed and move around. Taking a shower is just too much trouble, and I don't want to do that either. I really need help." She told her daughter to get her things, and they were leaving. "Right now?"

"Yes. I'm going to get you some help. Right now." She didn't know what to do, but going to the emergency room to get help seemed like a good start. "We'll have one of the family members pick me up if they want to keep you—no, I'm going to insist that they keep you to help you. I don't think I'll be fit to drive home after that."

"Mom, you're really going to do this? Take me to the hospital?" She said that was the only place that she could think of that would help them all. Lynn started crying, but her smile was what she focused on the most. "Thank you, Mom."

When Lynn reached behind her and then laid a handgun on the dresser beside them, Chalina stared at it while Lynn told her what she was going to do. She had planned it out to the second, it seemed.

"When you were with Saul tonight, I was going to go out into the yard and end my life. I stole this from Grandda Clarence's house a month ago to die then, but then I got hurt. Now, more than ever, I just want to be gone from this world and just be dead. I can't stand the pain in my mind and heart when I think of everything, all the things that have happened to me." Before she could think of how it might hurt her daughter, she told her she was selfish. "I am. I know that."

They drove to the hospital, not saying much. She couldn't contact Saul yet. Her heart was feeling ripped apart, but she knew that he was going to have to be there for her. When he contacted her, asking her what was going on, he said he could feel her pain. She told him everything.

"*I'll meet you at the hospital.*" She said that she needed that. "*Honey, just be calm and let her do the talking. She might only be a child, but she would know the answers to anything they ask her more than you would. You might not be able to stay with her once you get there. They'll want to establish that she'd not doing this because you told her to. All right?*"

"*Yes. I understand. She had a gun, Saul. She was going to leave us tonight.*" He said that he was nearly there. "*All right. I think that the others need to know, but I don't want them...this is hers, and they'll need to wait on answers before coming here.*"

"*I'm talking to my dad. He's with me. I've just pulled in. Thankfully, I didn't get pulled over.*" Almost as soon as the woman behind the desk asked if they were wanting to be seen, Lynn started talking. Some of the things she told the woman hurt her heart. Her little girl had been depressed like this for so long. She'd been thinking about it since she was a child.

Lynn was taken away from her. Chalina remained at the desk with the woman because she wanted Saul to be able to see her first thing. As soon as he came through the doors, she ran to him and his dad, crying and babbling about how brave Lynn was.

"She'll be all right, honey. You wait and see." She wanted to believe Joseph, but her heart was hurting. All she could think about was that she'd had a gun for a month and could have used it at any time. That scared her more than anything.

The entire family showed up, and for once, she was glad that they'd not listened to her. It was great having the support. Caitlynn took charge of the situation and got them in to see Lynn being assigned to her room and given scrubs to put on. It broke her in ways that she couldn't put words to that her daughter looked so small on the hospital bed that she was going to have to leave her care to someone else for a change. After that, they all sat down and spoke to the doctor once Lynn was put on some medications to help her relax.

Doctor Bruce asked her and Saul some questions; however, the entire family had answers for him. Did they ever see Lynn hurting herself? Did she act out enough that they'd had to spank her? The man was very thorough, and at one point, Chalina said she needed a break. Saul followed her out of the room.

"She's going to all right, won't she?" He said that he had all the faith in the world in her getting better, even if she needed to be on medication for the rest of her life. "I missed it all. I didn't see any of it."

"She's been hiding it all her life. Lynn has gotten really good at hiding in plain sight. But she's asked for help, and now we're going to get her the best care we can. We'll get her the best of care no matter the cost." She laid her head on his chest and hugged him. She's going to need all of us to help her. That much I learned from a guy I went to school with. Family support will be what she needs most of all."

"I don't want to leave her, but I know that I will have to. Do you think they'll watch her closely?

They won't allow her to hurt herself, will they?" He said that they'd be watching her better than they could. "I don't know how that is possible, but I'm glad she's going to be taken care of."

Going back into the room, the doctor pushed a bottle of medication to her. When she picked it up, reading the name on the bottle, she asked him what it was for. He smiled before speaking.

"You. And I want you to use it too. It'll give you a way to sleep better at night instead of up all night worrying. You won't be able to help her if you're sick, and she's going to need all of your help." The doctor smiled at her again. "I have to tell you something, Mrs. Tate. You did a good job raising Lynn and giving her a family like the Tates to depend on. Most kids her age don't go to someone when they're dealing with depression. They just do what they think is the best way of dealing with things, and it's too late. She went to you and told you that she had a problem. That speaks volumes for how loved and secure she feels for the family dynamics that she's living in. You're not to blame for her feeling the way that she does, either."

"I feel like I failed her." He told her that she'd

not failed her at all but had done something about it right away when she spoke to her. "She said she wanted help, and this was all I could think to do."

"Which is perfectly the correct thing you should have done. You didn't know how to fix this, so you found some way to make it work for her. The most important thing you did for her was to not blow it off or tell her she was too young to be depressed. She had a gun. She wasn't too young to figure that out. From what she told me, you didn't hesitate a second to get her here. That, my dear woman, saved her life. Don't you ever think otherwise. She would have ended her life tonight just as she had planned." Nodding and dealing with the pain in her heart, she asked what they were going to be doing for her. "Nothing for now. Watching her so that she gets what she needs at first. We're going to observe her and figure out what is making her so depressed. It could be mental, or it might be chemical. She could just need some medications or therapy, too. Whatever she needs, we'll figure it out with her help."

On their way home that night, staying in the apartment like they'd planned, she took two of the Xanax as prescribed and did feel it start to work for her immediately. Falling asleep quickly, she knew that Saul would watch over them both until they could go and see Lynn again.

Chapter 7

When the prison called and asked if they would claim Chad's body, instead of having him cremated and his ashes flying all over the place when he dumped them out, he asked to have his body taken to the farm. He knew a great deal about the Body Farm and was glad that someone somewhere was going to get some use of Chad now that he was dead. It was, he thought, the first decent thing he'd done since he'd been born.

About an hour after he told the prison what to do with him, he got a call from the Farm. They wanted questions answered about the state of the body as well as if they had any timeline that they needed to follow. He told them briefly who and what he'd done to be put in prison, and they were thrilled to have a fresh body and how he'd been killed. Saul was happy about that. One less thing that he'd have to worry about with all the other things going on.

He'd used the body farm before for deaths in the pack. Some of the older pack members hadn't ever had a birth certificate because they were either born at home or abandoned after birth. It happened a good deal more than it did nowadays. Someone would pass on, and there would be no record of their lives but for the people that they spent time with in a pack.

Using the body farm, a place that would lay out bodies or body parts to see how they would decompose after death, was a good way to help a lot of agencies. They would, at times, take a body, hang it from a tree like it had been caught up in the limbs, and the person died—from broken bones or starvation. It would depend on what the body had died from in real life. Some of the bodies that were out there, he'd heard, were decades old. Helping with forensics with the information that they got, they could tell the state of bodies in different situations at different times in the different stages of decomposition.

After telling Chalina that things were taken

care of with Chad, she didn't ask him what he'd done but thanked him for taking care of it. He was fine with that. It would add to her nightmares if she had any kind of inkling as to what was going to happen to his body after death.

Getting his desk cleared off made him happy. There were several projects that he was able to sign off on and three more that he could finally get someone to start on. They tried hard as a company to only have a few things going on at once. It saved them time from running all over the state, and it was also easier to keep up with them if they didn't have to run in different directions to keep up with the pace of what was going on. When Joel joined him in his office, he asked him about the one project that they'd been putting off for weeks now.

"You didn't get back to me on it, so I've left it where it is. I have recently put the specs on paper. The costs have risen, just like everything else has, so we'd have to recalculate those again. But other than that, it's not been touched." Joel asked him how long it would take him to get the revised prices. "No more than an hour. We cut a deal with two companies when we started out on pricing. However, if they want to jack their prices up too much, we'll have to start over to find a new supplier."

Joel got up to pace. When he did that, Saul knew that he was going to be tossing out ideas that he thought of but nothing that Saul had to worry about. When he stopped abruptly, it startled Saul enough that he looked around at what might have made him stop.

"Three weeks ago, remember that man that came to the office and asked us to give them some money that they could use to upgrade their church? I think you were with me. If not, then it was Dad. Do you remember?" He shook his head. "All right. Can you start looking at prices for the project I was talking about while I get Dad here?"

"Sure. What's this all about? If I remember correctly, these were two different projects." Joel told him that he thought that they were as well until this morning. "Okay. I'll get a start on it now. You contact Dad."

Saul was nearly finished with the new numbers by the time their dad came to the offices. To bring a peace offering, Dad had picked up lunch for the three of them, and he found out later that Dad had been the one who had brought the other project up and was fussing about it. But Saul had also been able to talk to Chalina and Layton about the project that he was working on for them. This was why he hated it when they were all going in several directions. It was as if he had to have knowledge of each of them so they'd not get pissy with him.

He ate his lunch while the other two were talking about the price difference. Saul was also trying to remember what the project was about that Dad and Joel were talking about with the other man while he answered questions for Jeremiah. He wanted blocks for his classroom to build on the playground with.

"What kind of blocks?" He told him that if he were to get raw blocks, he could have them sanded and painted by the time that school started again. "No, I mean size. I should have been more clear. You don't want boulder-sized blocks, I'm sure."

"Yeah, one or two of them to be climbed on. I have an idea to put ladders on them so that kids can get on top of them to build. Remember how much fun we used to have when we were kids playing king on the mountain? I loved that. I'm thinking that if I could get a couple of good-sized blocks for them to climb and then build on, it would be something that would last for a while, too." He smiled, remembering how much fun they really had doing that. "Mr. Jones said that he could set them in concrete so that the kids can't move them. I think that's a brilliant idea. If we could get them for free, that would make them even better."

"There is a place out on Forty called Stave Builders. They use trees to make barrels for whiskey. I'm sure that they don't use all the trees when they cut them down. Let me give them a call and see what I can find out. Also, if I remember correctly, they also cut down the bark to use for roofing. I don't remember how it works, but I know that they do that." Jeremiah asked if he could call him. "That would be fantastic. I have too much going on right now and was going to tell you that I won't get to it until later."

"I'll make the call. I think I might know one of them. Micky Stave and I went to school together. It might be the same family." After giving his brother the number, he put the phone back on his desk. Dad and Joel were getting kind of loud, and

he was having to move his work to the other side
of the room to be able to hear.

Just as he was getting ready to get their
attention, Caitlynne came in and let go of a loud,
ear-piercing whistle that got all their attention. She
winked at him when he thanked her.

"Joel, I said if you give me just a minute, I'd
find the man's name. It's William Couch. When I
found it, I ran a quick check on him, and he was
not a reverend of any kind. I don't know if that's
important or not, but there is a warrant out for his
arrest for illegal parking at the store across from
this office." Joel asked her what that had to do
with anything. "Nothing. I was just enjoying the
quiet with you two, not arguing anymore, and I
thought that I'd fill the silence a little more. Couch
is looking for donations to have a church built. I
don't know if you guys normally help with that
sort of thing, but I believe, from what I've been able
to find out with just a light search, that we don't
want to involve ourselves in his sort of religion.
He believes in sacrifices. As in, his congregation
cuts off their own body parts to burn in a fire
when the church is praying for something to come
their way." He asked her if she was joking. "No.

I wish I was. But just three months ago, he and his followers were run out of town when they cut the foot off of a ten-year-old little boy to use. His parents were going to reap the payments—no, I don't know what that might have been, but he wasn't a willing participant. The kid got someone to help him get to the police, and they arrested his mom and dad. The kid had a list of missing sisters that had been used, too. Apparently, the larger the need, the more they have to cut off."

"Christ." Caitlynn nodded at Dad. "That Couch person, he was just telling me that he has such a following—oh, I think I'm going to be sick."

Dad ran to the bathroom, and they could hear him retching. As usual, they felt the need to throw up as well. Going to the window in his office, he was able to sit in the cool breeze. When Dad came back with a cup of water, he asked him if he was all right.

"No, I ain't all right. They're…well, someone needs to call the police. He's down there talking the arm off of Chalina and Hanna. I ain't worried about those girls. They can handle him, but what they do to him is the kicker. Get him arrested, Joel, before—" Dad ran to the bathroom again.

He'd not realized that his dad had such a delicate belly. Of course, they'd never discussed people cutting up other people to use to pray or whatever he was doing with it. Saul stayed by the window and watched as the police gathered up in their cars and were headed out of town. He'd bet in five minutes, they'd be returning with their man in custody. He told the room of people that the police were on their way.

"I hope they don't make it. Hanna knows now, and she's fit to be tied. Woo hoo, I'd hate to be that man waiting on the police. Them girls will have him tied up and singing what he'd done in no time." His dad certainly had a way with words.

The police were back in about twenty minutes. Joel was giving them a blow-by-blow accounting of the situation at the house. Apparently, Chalina was smacking the man around, and Hanna was holding him upright with her magic so that she could get better angles on his head and face. When he got out of the cruiser once they were able to put him in cuffs, Couch looked like he'd gone a round or two with a prizefighter, and he didn't come out on top.

After having a good few laughs about Couch,

they were able to get back to work. He'd been right in the thing between the church and Joel's project. They didn't have anything to do with one another. Couch had approached Dad, and that reminded him that they'd not gotten back to him. Joel wanted to get the project that he'd been started on in the works again.

After everyone left, Chalina joined him to work on some of the projects that needed to be filed away. Saul had someone to do that, but he knew that Chalina needed to keep herself busy while Lynn was away. They had both talked to her last night, and it made them both cry a little, but she seemed to be doing better, and that's what made her being there worth it.

"Lynn had her doctor call me today. She wants me to bring her some more pants to wear around the floor. I told her that we'd pick them up and bring them by tomorrow. Is that all right with you?" He told her that he didn't mind that at all. "I didn't think you would. Also, she wants some composition notebooks. I had to look them up because I remembered what I needed in English class, but she said she wanted some pretty ones. Remember them from school? They were these oddly colored black and white books with composition written on the front. I guess they're prettier now."

"When school supplies are put out at the end of summer, I did notice them then. They're still the same odd drawing but in different colors. Did she say what colors she wanted?" He was about half paying attention to Chalina as he was thinking about Joel's project that he was working on. He looked up at her when she didn't answer him. "I'm sorry. Joel has this idea that the elementary school could be used for an office building. We had it earmarked for a halfway house at one time. I don't think that is going to work either. Then I thought of what Lynn was talking about doing with it, and I was trying to remember the details about it, too."

"What did she want to do with it?" Chalina sat down in the chair that was near the window in his office. "I'm sure that she had all the details all laid out. Tell me what it is."

"An indoor craft mall. Each person would be responsible for their own room and money." He watched Chalina. "I missed something you said, didn't I. I'm sorry about that. I was actually thinking that I'd like to do one of her projects so she has something to work with when she gets home." She smiled at him. "Are you going to tell me, or do I have to tickle it out of you."

"I said that I'm going to have a baby. Your baby. I was wondering how you'd feel about it when you just mentioned how you had two projects to go over, and it didn't look like you were ever going to get them done. You're very distracted today. Why?" She was going to have a baby, was all he could think about now. "You're paying attention now, aren't you?"

"I am. Who told you that you were going to have a baby? I'm sure that you didn't go to the doctor." She said that Hanna told her. "I thought it would be her or Cody. They seemed to be the most in—how do you feel about having our baby? Do you feel all right?"

"I do, actually. I didn't tell Lynn. I nearly did, but I think that she has enough going on right now without adding a little sister or brother to the lot. What do you think?" He said he didn't know, but it might be something she'd be happy about. But I don't know. It also might be a trigger for her, too."

"I'll talk to her doctor. He seems like he's

doing a good job with her, don't you think? I mean, Lynn talks about their sessions like she's enjoying them." Saul said that he thought that just having someone to talk to who doesn't judge or try to help is something that she needed. "Yes, I was too helpful sometimes. Or, as Lynn told me, my too helpfulness wasn't helping her at all. She couldn't think. Sometimes I feel like I've really screwed up with her. Other times, I feel like I failed her. It's never anything that I've had to think about before. Now, it's all I can think about."

"Have you given any more thought to seeing someone yourself? I know that the doctor suggested a couple of other doctors for you." She turned in her chair so that her legs were hanging off the side, much like he'd seen Lynn do when she was thinking. "I will do whatever you need, honey. But you're still having nightmares, and that worries me."

"The dreams, the nightmares are different now. They're scary, but...I think about that gun that Lynn had. And where she got it from. Mostly, what she said to me concerning the gun and her plans to use it. Turning it over to the police made me feel better, but I feel like I should have noticed that she had it sooner. Don't you think?" He asked her if she'd gotten the feeling that Lynn needed to use it. "You mean, did I think she was depressed like that? Then no. I didn't have…did I not have any idea, Saul, or did I not want to see it? That's what scares me the most. I missed it."

"I wish I could tell you what you need to hear, but honey, I just don't know that much about depression or suicidal thoughts. I never noticed it, but I didn't know Lynn before she came here. She was a little testy, but I just wrote that off as being nearly a teenager. Did I notice that she was down, suicidal? No. I didn't. I've asked around, too, but no one in this family has ever thought that. But the doctor did tell us that she had been hiding it since she was a baby. She'd had a great deal of practice at hiding her feelings." Chalina kicked her feet, another thing that Lynn did when she was thinking. "You remember what Sherm said to us? How she might well have thought that her feelings and thoughts were normal. Then she met him and realized—she even told him that. That he wasn't like her when it came to being a person. He didn't understand until it came about that she was fighting some very nasty demons."

"When I spoke to her this morning, she seemed just like she always did. Happy, funny. I didn't know if those were her true feelings or not. I guess I'm going to have to take what I can get from her, aren't I? Learn her too." She looked at him. "I want her here with me so that I can hug all those thoughts out of her. But I also know that it wouldn't be enough. I'd be too much for her. So she's safer where she is, getting help from people who can see what none of us did."

"That's right. It is good too that she is getting help." Saul watched Chalina. For the past several days, she'd been crying a great deal. He knew that she didn't think he knew it, but he always knew when she was upset. After he'd spoken to the doctor about it, he told him just to be there when she wanted to talk. Not to offer advice, just to answer questions as well as he could and let her deal with whatever she was thinking on her own. Unless it was something that might harm her. He didn't want her to be harmed in any way, so it was difficult for him to let her work things out for herself.

"I'm going to get help. If for no other reason than I can deal with the demons, as you called them, when they come up. Having you around, even if it's in the other room, you've no idea how much that helps me. Even just knowing that you're in the other room gives me a boost to my heart that you can't even imagine." He told her that he loved her. "And I love you. So very much, Saul. Wanna fool around?"

"Always." He picked her up out of the chair and carried her to the stairs. Kissing her lightly on the mouth, he told her that she was going to have to be less of a distraction from now on, or he was going to have to hire someone to come in and clean up his messes when he wanted to make love to her. "You're a very nice distraction."

"Thank you. You are the best kind of distraction, too."

~*~

Once he got her in their room, he sat her on her feet. There was something so wonderful about having someone love you and want to make love whenever the mood hit them. Laying her over the bed, she pulled the sheet over her body when she was suddenly nude.

Saul told her that he wanted a word with his child. Kissing her belly, then laying his head there, he told the little person that he was going to love them forever and a day. Then he made his way down to Chalina's pussy and laid his head there. Using his chin to bring her to her peak, it thrilled him to no end to watch her face while she enjoyed herself.

Saul moved against her pussy again and again, the friction taking them both higher and higher. He wanted to topple over the edge and get satisfaction before he hurt her, claiming her again. Taking in a deep breath, he cried out when she spoke.

"Please, Saul, please, take me now." Her voice purred at him. She could do that so well, call out to him with her needs, and he had little choice but to give her anything and everything that she wanted. And would forever.

With each of his downward strokes, she moved up, driving him on. He wanted her with a desperate need and knew as soon as he gave in, they would come together hard and fast. The need to reclaim what was his soared through him in that moment, making thinking about anything else but her impossible. Christ, he loved this woman. It was like each time he touched her, he needed to make her his. To claim not just her heart but her body as well.

Saul slid down her body, biting her nipple through her shirt that barely covered her, soaking it as he tried to pull her breast into his mouth. Her body arched into his, giving him more of her breast to suckle. Her whimpering was becoming loud and repetitive, like a siren's call to his needs. She was wet and hot. He could smell her perfumed scent of need on his tongue.

"Chalina, love, I want you again. I need to be inside of you. But I want to taste you first." He barely recognized his own voice. It was deep and raspy with need. "I want you to come down my throat. Please, baby. It's all I can think of right now."

Saul tugged at her covering, tearing it away in his haste to pull her bared flesh into his mouth to toy with her hard nipple with his tongue. His cock was throbbing and tight, the blood beating hard and fast through him like his heart was. He moved down and settled himself between her legs.

"Bend your knees, spread them wide for me. I want to taste you. I want to lick your pussy and have you come in my mouth while I do it."

He watched her face while she moved to do what he wanted. When she had her legs spread as wide as they would go, he inserted a finger deep into her pussy, fucking her like that until he could gather his control. Laughing slightly, he knew that he'd lost all sense of control the moment he'd met her.

Her hips came up off the bed, grinding into his mouth with each stroke of his fingers. Her pussy wept for him, soaking his fingers and his hand with her hot juices. He could even feel it running down his chin.

Spreading her thighs wider open for him, Chalina looked down at him with anticipation as his warm breath caressed her throbbing clit. As he moved his mouth closer to his treasure, she moved up to meet him. He ran his tongue along the seam of her nether lips, gathering the cream that was now pooling onto the sheets beneath her. She screamed out his name, bucking up and down the moment he touched her. He flicked his tongue against her clit quickly, making her shudder hard against his mouth.

"Please." Her begging came out in a long hiss. She wanted his mouth on her and grabbed his head to show him.

He fucked her pussy with his tongue and fingers, his tongue lapping her up and his fingers touching and stroking her sweet spot inside of her. She was close, so very close, and he wanted her to come, wanted to taste her when she did. He continued to lick and suckle her clit, loving the way her body rocked against his face. Her juices leaking onto the bed each time he sucked a little harder.

"Come for me, Chalina. I want you to come. I want to taste your cum in my mouth, down my throat. Come for me, baby, now!"

He increased his pace, sucking harder and pumping his fingers in and out of her. Drawing her clit into his mouth and bit gently. Her climax ripped through her and into him. He could only hold onto her and ride wave after wave of her orgasms, feasting on the copious amount of hot cream filling him. With the last of her tremors still subsiding, he crawled up her body, tearing the sheet away and anything else that she might have had on her when she'd come into their room. Closing his eyes, he feasted on her breast, suckling first one, then the other, then nipping at her nipples until she was at a fevered pitch again. Leaning back on his heels, he began stroking his cock, fisting it hard while he watched her beneath hooded eyes.

"You like this, don't you? You like me stroking my cock for you, don't you?" He asked her, looking at her with heavily lidded eyes. He didn't want to hurt her, but he knew that if he did, she'd come hard. He knew that if he entered her now, there would be no gentleness between them. Too much had happened to them, and his need to assert himself as her mate was driving him over the edge.

"Yes. Please, Saul, inside of me, please. I want to feel you come inside of me." He wanted to come and come all over her body. Her hands were pulling at him, his hair and skin, to get him closer to her. Inside of her.

Saul stroked up and down once more, then leaned into her and entered her core just as he had been thinking about for days now. One thing or another kept them apart, but no more. He was going to claim her as his, and there was going to be no stopping him from doing it. Suddenly, he wanted to taste her throat, needed to sink his teeth into her flesh like his wolf would when he took her. As he pushed just enough to enter her, he licked the pulse. He felt her shudder and tighten. He pushed forward, completely burying both his cock and his teeth into her, sinking deep into her flesh, tasting her blood as it filled his mouth.

As soon as he drew his first taste of her into his mouth, he felt her tighten around him, pulling him deeper into her, her climax immanent. He began to move within her, his hips slapping against hers in a primal rhythm that echoed through the room.

"Chalina... Gods, you feel so..." he groaned, his eyes closed in ecstasy.

Her nails dug into his back as she met him thrust for thrust, their bodies moving in perfect harmony as if they were meant to be together forever. Suddenly, her arms wrapped around him, pulling him closer to her breast and her pounding pulse. He felt his body responding to hers. His balls tightened up against him, on the verge of his own climax. He knew he was close too when his movements became more frantic, his thrusts deeper and harder. He could feel himself swelling inside her, ready to explode again.

"Wait, not yet. Please, not yet." She begged

him. He nearly cried out in frustration. What could there be that she wanted him to wait for?

Then he felt it, something moving from him to her, through him, over her. He pulled harder on her breast, drawing more of her essence into him through her throat. Suddenly, his heart began to pound, beating hard like it was going to leap from his chest. Chalina's scream shattered through him.

"Saul, come now! Please, I need for you to take me and make me all yours." He didn't need to be asked twice. As soon as he released, his body seemed to pause, like his heart needed to catch up with the pounding in his ears. Then it happened.

His release was instantaneous, both of them coming together and apart at the same time. He pulled away from her, and he threw back his head and roared. It echoed throughout the room, blending with hers a symphony of sexual completion. Nothing like this had ever happened to him before, and he knew, on some level, it would never happen again, either.

Dropping atop her, he felt a tingling in his fingers when he stretched out his hands. Like he'd been holding too tightly on something, her body and the blood had been used for something else.

His epic climax. Their epic releases.

It was ten minutes before either of them could move or even wanted to. He knew that he was heavy on top of her but could not gather the energy to roll to his side.

When he finally did, he moved to his back, dragging her over him, pulling her close, securing her to his body by wrapping her in his arms. They slept like that, neither of them moving throughout the rest of the night and the entire next day, stirring only when the sun went down the next evening. He had never felt so rested in his life when he woke up.

Starving, he made his way to the kitchen after his shower. Chalina wouldn't allow him to shower with her, so he took his first and let her soak while he got dressed. Then he went to find something to eat. Christ, he felt wonderful. He didn't know if it was being in love or the fact that he was going to be a dad.

He had to hold onto the wall when it occurred to him that he was going to be a dad again. A dad who would be as happy as ever anyone could be if he got a little boy this time. Children were the lifeline of his life, and he couldn't have been happier than he was right now.

Chapter 8

School started in two days, and Jeremiah had never been so excited for the return of the kids. The area where the murders had been committed was no longer the cafeteria but a meeting room for those kids who had a free period. It had been decorated with a trophy cabinet, something that they'd never had before, as well as a huge chalkboard that could be used by the students to say whatever they wanted. It was cleaned off each Friday night after school, and he just hoped that no one abused the board by writing things that weren't appropriate.

Even though the classes here were kindergarten through sixth grade, he knew that someone sometime was going to abuse the board. He only hoped that it wouldn't happen too often.

"Mr. J?" He turned when he heard the voice

behind him. Smiling, he asked the young man if he would help him. "I think so. I'm new to this area, and my dad is working. Is it all right that I get registered so I can start when school opens up again?"

"We can get most of the paperwork started, but your dad will need to sign off on a few things, too. You can take them home with you and get them fixed up if that will help him." The boy, about eight or nine, said that would be great. "All right. You have a seat there, and I'll see what I can figure out for you. I've only been principal for about a month now, so I'm learning too."

"My cousin goes here. Well, she did. Now she goes to the middle school. Her name is Darcy James. Her mom and dad are getting a divorce. My aunt has decided that she likes girls as her wife." He looked confused for a moment. "I don't know what that means, but she said that she's happier now that she's found someone to love her. I'm going to miss her being around."

Jeremiah had to stifle a laugh. The kid was going to be in trouble if he kept telling family secrets like that one. After finding the notes on what was needed for the boy to register to go to school, he found out his name was Cody Mann, and he was nine.

Before they were finished up with what he could fill out about the boy, Jeremiah had laughed more than he had in a long time. He was a delightful kid, and he enjoyed his honesty. He was sure that his family wouldn't, but he was happy to have him as a distraction for the afternoon.

"I've put tabs where your dad needs to sign the paperwork. Also, a list of things that you're going to need to bring in your first day of school." Cody said he would get them. Just as he was seeing the little boy out of the building, Hanna appeared in the lobby of the doors and put her hand on Cody. He didn't move or finish the sentence that he'd been saying.

"His name isn't Cody Mann. He doesn't have any parents around here, as he's been on the run for a while now. He's a runaway who is better off without his family than most people are with them." He asked her what he needed to do. "Nothing for now. Just take him back to the office, say you forgot something, and you'll keep him safe."

"What are you going to do to them?"

She simply smiled at him, but it was far from a friendly-looking one and not very reassuring, either. "Hanna, if you get hurt because of this, my brother is going to strip my hide. You know that, don't you?"

"Your brother is at the moment taking care of the father. I'm going to go to the mother, a pillar of good standing she is not, and take care of her." He opened his mouth to ask what they were going to do when she cut him off. He knew this couldn't be good. "Don't ask, Jeremiah. The less you know, the better."

"All right. I'm going to trust you on this. When you ask me to keep him here, I'm assuming that they've figured out where he is. Will me taking him back to my office keep him from getting harmed?" She told him he would be harmed, but he'd not die from it. He raised an eyebrow at that comment, then folded his arms across his chest. "That's not very encouraging. You know that, don't you?"

"Go to your office. I swear to you that he'll not die. Hurt? Yes, but he will not die." Nodding, she disappeared, and Cody finished his question.

He placed his hand on the kid's shoulder. "I

forgot something to give you. Can you come back to the office with me for a minute?" He nodded and followed him. Jeremiah turned and looked at him. "Look, kid. I know your name isn't Cody and that you're on the run. My sister-in-law just told me. We're going to go into the boys' room, the only place I can think of that might keep you safe. All right?"

"They're here?" He told the boy that he didn't know where they were but that she had told him that he might be hurt. Instead of telling him that he was going to be hurt, he didn't think the little lie would hurt either of them. Besides, going to his office might well be the—he remembered something that he'd been told a while back.

"We're going to my office. That's where Hanna told me to go. I'm afraid if I do something different than that, something might change the outcome. We'll go to my office, but I want you to sit on the floor under my desk. It's the best place I can think of that might keep you safer." He told him he'd gladly do that. "We're going to be honest with each other from now on. First things first, what is your real name? And anything else that you told me that you fibbed about, I want the truth."

"My name is Richard Stonehouse. I am nine years old. The people looking for me aren't my parents. I was kidnapped from my parents when I was a baby. They took me so that they'd have a kid to get food stamps for me being there." He thanked him for that. "You should also know that my real parents are both gone. They were killed by the couple that took me."

When he started to cry, Jeremiah held him tightly. He didn't understand people like the ones that were in his family. Why would they have children if all they were going to do to them was abuse and hurt them? When Richard pulled away, he let him. Not saying a word to him, he handed him a box of tissues and pulled out his chair to let him hide under his desk.

Almost as soon as he was under the desk, Jeremiah's door burst open, and an animal—he really didn't know what else to call the person who came in with a gun in her hand—came into his office demanding to know where her boy was.

"I'm sorry, but I don't know who your boy is. Not to mention, you can see that the room is empty but for the two of us." She told him that she knew that he was hiding him. "Who?"

"My son, you moron. Where is he? The little fucker ran off, and I want him back." Again, he told her that he didn't know what she was talking about. "Well, how about I shoot you full of holes, and you suddenly remember where he is? That sounds like a good plan, don't you think?"

"If you shoot me full of holes, I'm reasonably sure that I'm going to be dead and of no help to you at all. Not that I would help you, what with you carrying around a gun. But I don't know who your son is nor where he would be if I knew him. For all I know, you're going to kill whoever your son is for running off." He reached out to Hanna to tell her what was going on. She told him to hang tight and keep her talking. "Why don't you tell me who you are and what your son's name is, and perhaps I can look on the roster to see if he'd enrolled here. That's the only reason that I can think of why you'd come here, and that's because you know that he goes to school here."

"Are you that dumb?" He asked her what she meant. "If I tell you his name, you're going to tell the police. I don't want that."

"Then how do you expect me to tell you where

he is if I don't know his name? This conversation is getting stupider with every word that comes out of your mouth." She looked confused, and he decided he was going to talk over her head until she left. "Registration is a family thing, so I don't know how he would have gotten to be here if I didn't know that he's registered. Obviously you had nothing to do with him being here at this school if you don't even know his name. Which I'm thinking is grounds for me not telling you if he's here or not. Not that I could because, apparently, you don't even know his name. You don't, do you?"

"What are you talking about? Of course, I know his name. He's my kid, isn't he?" Jeremiah said that he didn't have any idea if she had a son or not. "I do have one. Damn it, you're confusing me."

He heard Hanna laughing through their link, and it made him grin a little, too. Richard wrapped his arms around his leg when he sat down in his chair. This was fun, he thought. Even though she had a gun waving it around, he wasn't worried the least bit about her killing him. However, he did worry about Richard.

"What's his name and I'll look him up?" She sat there for a few seconds and then confessed, stupidly, if you asked him, that she didn't remember what his name was this time. "I'm sorry, what? You don't know his name this time? What the heck does that mean? You change his name all the time?"

"I didn't say that. I know it. I just don't want to tell you what it is." Hanna told him that they change it every time they move around. Last month, it was Rachel James. He started to ask her if that was a girl's name.

"She didn't know how to spell anything else and wrote the name of the person who was helping her fill out the food stamp information. She's as dumb as a post, isn't she? I need her to say something about the boy that is hiding. Good thought that, putting him under the desk. If you speak to him through a link, he'll hear you. I've made it so that he can hear me, too." He thanked her for that and realized that he'd missed something dumbass was saying. Asking her to repeat herself, she huffed and actually stomped her foot at him.

"I said, you need to tell me where he is before I shot you up." He pulled up his email and looked over one that she could read. There wasn't all that much, but he also figured that since she couldn't read, he'd be safe. "What are you doing there? You'd better not be typing to the police."

"I don't think they have an email address that calls them in. I was looking for the roster and going to let you read it over to see if you can find his name." She told him that wouldn't work for her. "And why is that? You want to find him, don't you?"

"You're driving me nutty." He said he thought she was already nutty. "What did you just say to me? You're going to get yourself shot up full of holes if you keep that up."

"Do you have a thing about shooting people up full of holes? I mean, you keep saying that. Like it's a big threat. I doubt that if I was your son and you couldn't remember my name, I'd be hiding from you too." She told him to shut up. "No. I'm done talking to you. I think it's time you leave, or you're going to piss me off, and I'm going to hurt you. Notice how I said hurt you and didn't mention shooting you full of holes? Anyway, I'm a wolf shifter. If you keep sitting there, I'm going to shift and tear your throat out. I've had enough of your crap today."

He let himself go. It wasn't hard, but it did have him ending up on the desk rather than on the floor like he thought he'd land. But it had the effect that he wanted; the woman started screaming and yelling about him going to eat her, and he was glad to hear her dry-shooting the gun. It was, as he'd thought, not loaded.

Leaping at her, he was careful that he didn't unsheathe his claws. He didn't want to kill her, just scare her. Having her arrested was much better than dead. There was enough death in this building to last several lifetimes.

The police entered just as her chair fell backwards, hitting her head on the floor. She was out. Donnie, a good friend of his on the force, was laughing too hard to speak to him, but he finally understood that he needed to shift and get ready for the other officers. Going to his own bathroom, he did shift and was surprised that he was dressed. Coming out, he was asked to have a seat so that he could be asked some questions.

"I have the boy." Donnie asked him if he'd been in here all the time. "Yes. I didn't want him to get hurt, so I distracted the woman enough that she didn't get up and look around for him. He's under my desk. Come out, Richard."

The boy leapt at him, hugging him tightly as the woman that had pretended to be his mom was handcuffed. She was still out, but they didn't want to take any changes with her being able to get up and move around. Thankfully, by the time the ambulance arrived, she was still out and going nowhere. It felt like he'd had a great day and didn't have to have anyone killed.

~*~

Chalina waited at the table for Lynn to come out and see her. She wasn't allowed to go beyond the doors, and she was all right with that for as long as she could see her. When she came down the hall, she noticed that she was on crutches and that her foot was in a cast. The nurse with her was laughing, so she didn't get very upset about what might have happened.

"I did it myself, Mom. I tripped over a chair and came down hard. I have to be more careful in the future about using my cane." They both sat down and the nurse, Lynn's personal nurse, Beth, moved away so that they could talk. "They said it was a clean break. I didn't want them to tell you because I felt silly. But I'm really all right. It hardly hurts anymore."

"You should heal quickly." Lynn nodded and looked with her to where two people were arguing about a game they were playing. "How has your week gone? Other than breaking your ankle? You look like you've lost some weight."

"I have. But not very much. The doctor told me that it was the medication. Once my body gets used to it, I'll be eating again. Mom, this place has the best food. Not like May's, our cook, but it's really good." Chalina handed her the tin of cookies that May had baked for her. "Oh, goodie. I'll share them at the next group meeting."

"How are things going? Do you need anything? I did bring you some pants, but they had to remove the tags and strings from them. I didn't think about that when I got them." They didn't want her to hang herself, so all things like that, strings, and buttons were removed before Lynn could have them. "I'll be better at it next time."

"You're doing great, Mom. I feel so much better knowing that I'm getting what I need. Not to mention, you guys coming to visit me all the time. I'm not going to tell you that you don't have to come so often because I love being able to show you the progress that I'm making, but you don't have to come so often if you have anything else to do."

"I don't. But to be with you." She thought of the baby she was carrying and remembered what the doctor had told her to do when she told her daughter. There were rules for everything, and she was glad to have them to follow. "How would you like being an older sister soon?"

"I thought you smelled different. I'm so happy for you." She asked her what she meant by her smelling. "You smell different. Earthy. I thought it was just me, but now that I know, I can smell that you're going to have a baby. Miss Beth is a wolf too, and she's telling me things that I can do now that I'm a wolf too. There was so much going on before that I didn't think to ask about stuff. I can dress myself too, but I have to be careful about that. The same with you having to remove the strings from my pants. I just have to be careful what I wear."

They talked about the things that were going on at home. Mostly, it was the family and what they were up to. Lynn seemed to be interested in everything, and she found that she was having too much fun telling stories about herself and the silly things she'd done since being married to Saul.

"We both miss you so much. I'm glad you're here, but I do miss you being here." Lynn smiled and said that she missed her as well. "Are you allowed to have a cell phone yet? I know they said that you might have to wait a little while."

"Not yet. It's because they don't want me to be able to look up things on the internet or get on social media. That's a big one. Although I can't see it, so I don't know what difference that makes." Her mom told her the videos on social media had sound. "I guess that makes sense. Miss Beth will allow me to use hers if I want to call you. But she has to clear it through my doctor first. I'm all right with that. I was on social media, and it's not good for people who are having trouble like I am. Not everyone is mean, but a lot of them are. So, I'm okay with not being on it. You know that having a link we can share would be the same as talking, right?"

"I know, but I'm afraid of interrupting something that you're doing." She told her that she'd tell her if she didn't have time to talk. "All right then, I'll make sure that I use it to talk to you.

Everyday. But you have to promise that you'll tell me if you get sick of hearing from me. All right?" Lynn promised.

"I'm going to be here for a while more. Did the doctor tell you that?" Chalina said that he'd spoken to both her and Saul. "He said that he would. I'm safer here. And I know that you don't want to hear this, but I'm still dealing with my killing myself. It's not as often, I swear, but here I can talk about it more. Like they're all in the same boat I am, and I can talk to them. There is even a doctor here in the middle of the night in the event someone needs him."

"I'm so happy for you, honey. Oh, before I forget, it's been cleared that Sherm comes to see you. He can only stay for an hour at a time, but he could come daily." She was so excited to hear that she was happy that she remembered. "He's been practicing brail for you. That kid is super smart, isn't he?"

"He is. There are times when he is dumb, too. But I love him so much. It's like the little brother I've never had." She smiled. "Or maybe my second little brother. I can't wait to see the baby. It'll be so cool when you bring him here."

She didn't let it bother her too much that Lynn was making plans to be here for a lot longer than she thought. Not that she'd drag her home or anything like that, but it did worry her that she was making long-term plans about—

"Mom, tell me what you're thinking. You have to do that too." She blurted out how she didn't like her staying here forever. "This is better than me being home and upset. I've grown up a lot while I've been here. If I have to stay forever, then I'll be all right with that. You guys should be, too. I have…I don't have everything that I need living here, but I feel better than I've felt in a long time. Like I don't ever have to hide away how I'm feeling. And I did that a lot. Faking my emotions, the doctor said, is what caused me to have so many troubles. I have to be more free with how I feel. Sometimes it hurts, but most of the time, I feel better when I talk to someone about my feelings and not be afraid that—not you, but some people won't tell me to blow it off or to snap out of it. My feelings are real, and they're mine. I need to own that, I was told."

When her time was up talking to Lynn, she hugged her several times and told her how much she loved her. She was barely to the car when she started crying. It hurt her to the very core that her daughter was taking her illness much better than she was. Her little girl was hurting, and she came to realize that there wasn't anything she could do about it unless she came to the realization that there wasn't anything that she could give her or make her do that would help. It was up to the doctors and nurses to make sure that she got what she needed.

She and Saul were going to dinner tonight with Joel and Caitlynne. Chalina wasn't too keen on going now, but she would. Caitlynne had become a very good friend, and if she needed to vent to anyone, it would be her.

All the women had become close, too. There were days that she didn't think she was going to get through the day without talking to one or all of them. As she drove herself home, Chalina heard from Hanna.

"I have a plan." That made her smile. Hanna's plans were slightly terrifying but fun. "You and I are going to take a trip to New York. I have to be there for business—don't ask what it is and after I'm finished with that, the two of us will go shopping. How does that sound?"

"Great. When do we leave?" She told her that since they didn't need to pack, they were going to leave as soon as she got home. "I have a date with Saul."

"Who do you think you'll have more fun with, him or me? Me. That's who. All right, we'll meet up at my house and go from there. I've already spoken to Saul, and he's fine with us leaving so long as you don't get hurt. Like I'd ever let that happen to my bestie."

By the time she was pulling into Hanna's house, their luggage, empty bags to bring stuff back in that were fun, she was ready to go. And Chalina was going to have a good time too. Even if she had to go on whatever mission Hanna was on to enjoy herself.

AWARD WINNING, BESTSELLING AUTHOR

Kathi Barton, a winner of the Pinnacle Book Achievement Award and a best-selling author on Amazon and All Romance books, lives in Nashport, Ohio, with her husband, Paul. When not creating new worlds and romance, Kathi and her husband enjoy camping and going to auctions. She can also be seen at county fairs with her husband, an artist and potter.

Her muse, a cross between Jimmy Stewart and Hugh Jackman, brings her stories to life for her readers in a way that has them coming back time and again for more. Her favorite genre is paranormal romance, with a great deal of spice. You can visit Kathi online and drop her an email if you'd like. She loves hearing from her fans. aaronskiss@gmail.com.

Follow Kathi on her blog: http://kathisbartonauthor.blogspot.com/